T0194154

Beach House REFUGE

A Love Story

Teresa Hartery

WESTBOW
PRESS®
A DIVISION OF THOMAS NELSON
& ZONDERVAN

Scripture quotations marked (ESV) are from the ESV® Bible (The Holy Bible,
English Standard Version®), copyright © 2001 by Crossway, a publishing
ministry of Good News Publishers. Used by permission. All rights reserved.

THE HOLY BIBLE, NEW INTERNATIONAL VERSION®,
NIV® Copyright © 1973, 1978, 1984, 2011 by Biblica, Inc.®
Used by permission. All rights reserved worldwide.

Scripture taken from the King James Version of the Bible.

Beach House Refuge is a work of fiction. Names, characters, places and
incidents are the product of the author's imagination or are used fictitiously. Any
resemblance to actual events, locales, or persons, living or dead, is coincidental.

WestBow Press books may be ordered through booksellers or by contacting:

WestBow Press
A Division of Thomas Nelson & Zondervan
1663 Liberty Drive
Bloomington, IN 47403
www.westbowpress.com
1 (866) 928-1240

Because of the dynamic nature of the Internet, any web addresses or
links contained in this book may have changed since publication and
may no longer be valid. The views expressed in this work are solely those
of the author and do not necessarily reflect the views of the publisher,
and the publisher hereby disclaims any responsibility for them.

Any people depicted in stock imagery provided by Thinkstock are models,
and such images are being used for illustrative purposes only.
Certain stock imagery © Thinkstock.

ISBN: 978-1-5127-8791-7 (sc)
ISBN: 978-1-5127-8790-0 (hc)
ISBN: 978-1-5127-8792-4 (e)

Library of Congress Control Number: 2017907881

Print information available on the last page.

WestBow Press rev. date: 05/18/2017

To my sweet and loving husband, Gary: your lighthearted approach to my novel and its characters was a delight as I completed this book.

To my longtime friend Shelley: you believed in my ability to pen this novel. Your encouragement inspired me to continue until completion.

Thank you both from the depths of my soul for your love and support throughout the long process of writing this book.

And warmest thanks to my readers.

Chapter 1

March 13, 2010
Little Gasparilla Island, Florida

As her fingers danced across the keyboard of her laptop, Tracie Lawrence suddenly realized that the words on the screen and the memory of that cold day in January seven years ago were identical. What had triggered her memory? Why was she typing the words that were not to be a part of this novel? It was like she was in a trance as she stared out at the ocean and watched the gentle waves lap the shore. She was working on the eighth chapter of her debut novel, which was a carefree, happily-ever-after story—nothing like the unwanted divorce she had gone through seven years earlier.

As she thought back to that time, she remembered that Nicholas had been acting very distant and quieter than usual. She had known something was troubling him. There were no telltale signs expect for his unusual quietness. He had gone about his normal activities, working, golfing, and watching his favorite shows on television. But he had not been his jovial self—no teasing, no joking around. All his responses to her questions were short and to the point, simply a yes or no answer where it applied. Every time Tracie had asked what was wrong, his response had always been the same: "Nothing."

On that particular morning, they had been having coffee by the fireplace. The only sound in the room was the crackling of the wood burning. Tracie had confronted him again.

"Nicholas, I don't know what's wrong, but I do know that something is certainly troubling you. You haven't been yourself for several weeks. I'm worried about you. Are you okay?" A long silence followed. When she looked over at him, his face held a stoic look. "What is it Nicholas?"

Finally, he said, "I'm not happy anymore."

"What—what do you mean?"

"Just that, Tracie. I'm not happy, and I haven't been for a long time."

Even though the fireplace held a blazing fire, the space around Tracie suddenly felt very cold. She didn't want to ask, but she had to. "Nicholas, are you seeing someone else?"

Again, silence followed. She had her answer.

Tracie looked back at the laptop screen. "Not sleeping well last night must be catching up with me," she said to herself. Since the divorce, she had spent most of her weekends at her aunt's beach house, and this weekend was no different. Although Aunt Betty was away visiting family, Tracie still had come to the island. The beach house had become her place of refuge for several years now.

She stood and stretched. "Come on, Max. Come on, boy. Let's go for a walk." Max, Tracie's dog, was a mixed breed, part border collie, part husky. His black-and-white coat was soft, shiny, and short. Tracie hadn't thought she could care so much for an animal. But after Nicholas had left, she'd rescued Max from a shelter. She had thought he would be good company, and it had turned out to be the best decision she had made in a long time. Max had truly become her best friend.

Max bounded ahead while Tracie slowed her pace. She was intrigued by all the shells and rocks that had washed up on the shore. She thought about how much they represented people. Some were beautiful with no blemishes. Some had a chip here, a crack there, or maybe a small hole, indicating that it may have had a slight challenge in making it to shore.

"Max, wait up, boy!" Tracie yelled as she pulled her gaze away from the shells and saw that he was getting a little too far ahead of her. She was sprinting to catch up to him, when he turned and ran back to meet her. "Good boy, Max, good boy." Oh, how she loved this dog! He really was a good boy. Most of the time, she only had to say something once, and he was obedient. She couldn't imagine how he'd ever ended up in a shelter.

They continued to walk, and Tracie let her mind wander back to the shells and rocks. The marks on the shells made her think of the different trials people went through. Some were minor setbacks, and some were major—and some devastated a person's very existence.

As Tracie let her mind wander, Max bounded on ahead again. She decided to sit and rest a bit. She had walked farther than she had intended. "Max, come here, boy." As soon as Max heard his name, he turned and headed back to where Tracie had already taken a seat on the sand. "Are you thirsty, boy?" Tracie asked, rubbing Max's ears. "Thank goodness I had the sense to grab the backpack with our water and snacks before we started walking." Tracie took Max's collapsible water bowl out of the backpack, popped it into shape, and poured water from her bottle into it before she took a long drink herself.

Max lay down beside Tracie in the sand, his head resting in her lap. She rubbed his ears and let her thoughts drift back to the shells and rocks. The waves pulling them back out to sea again and again reminded her of the pounding and the refiner's fire. The waves were the heat, the undertow pulling them back out, the pounding that removed the dross from precious gold.

As Tracie turned some shells and rocks over in her hand, she wondered why people's lives had different challenges, some more difficult or taxing than others. The shells, like people, each had a different character caused by the circumstances and trials they'd been handed to deal with in life.

Tracie thought that those who tossed and turned in the waves of life didn't experience the peace the ocean was supposed to bring. Rather, the waves brought turmoil to their life situations. Knowing that each wave could lead to another caused more emotional damage.

"So much for clearing my head, Max. At least I'm not thinking about the divorce anymore, huh, boy? We need to head back, Max. Time for lunch." With that, Max was off and running down the beach in the direction they had come.

Chapter 2

Aunt Betty was usually home when Tracie made her weekend visits, but this weekend Tracie had the place all to herself. Her aunt had taken off to the mountains of West Virginia to visit her brother Tom. Eighty-four-year-old Tom was the oldest of Tracie's dad's siblings. Her dad, John, was the middle child at age seventy-eight. And Betty, the youngest, was seventy-seven years old. Her grandmother had thought Tom would be an only child because she'd had three miscarriages by the time Daddy had been born six years later. Then, one year to the day after Daddy's arrival, Betty had come along. Grandma had said she was the most beautiful baby girl ever born, and she teased Daddy for years, telling him that Betty was his birthday present.

Aunt Betty didn't have any children of her own, so she had spoiled Tracie all her life. When Tracie was four, her mother had passed away. Aunt Betty was very sad, because Tracie's mom had been more of a sister to her than a sister-in-law. Aunt Betty was more than happy to help Daddy with the task of raising his little girl.

Though Betty was seventy-seven years old, she did not look or act her age. When she and Tracie went out to dinner or shopping together, they were often asked if they were sisters. Tracie was only fifty-two, and those comments would have made her feel old except for the fact that Aunt Betty looked quite young for her age. Betty was five feet seven inches tall, two inches taller than Tracie. She wore her hair short with feather-like bangs and always kept the most gorgeous auburn color on it. She would tell Tracie, "Just because you get old, you don't have to look old." She shared her soft skin secret with Tracie as well: "Pond's Cold Cream. Just a dab every evening before you go to bed. You don't need all those high-dollar products they have on the market today."

Aunt Betty's eyes were green, just like Tracie's. She wore just a touch of highlighter under her brows with a deep taupe shadow on her lids. She always wore black eyeliner and a light brush of black mascara. She never left home without her favorite apricot lip gloss. Aunt Betty always dressed in the latest fashions. She told Tracie, "You only feel as good as you look, so always try to look your best, even if you are spending the day at home."

With Aunt Betty gone this weekend, Tracie was left to fend for herself in the kitchen. When Tracie opened the refrigerator door, she was pleasantly surprised. She found a bowl of tuna noodle salad with grapes. Attached to the lid was a note from her aunt. "Thought you would enjoy this tuna salad for lunch after your morning on the beach. Hope it hits the spot. See you next weekend, sweetie. Love, Aunt Betty." Tracie smiled and said aloud, "You are so thoughtful, Aunt Betty. I don't know what I would do without you."

The beach house had a wonderful setup. There were two master bedrooms, each having a sitting area, an en suite, and a balcony. Tracie had claimed the one on the west side of the house for her own. She loved to sit on the balcony in the evening and watch the sunset. Aunt Betty preferred the one on the east side. She was an early bird and loved to watch the sunrise as she drank her coffee and had her morning devotions. Although Tracie only spent some weekends at the beach house, Aunt Betty had told her to decorate her space to her liking; but she still had not done anything to change the decor. Maybe once she finished her novel, she would concentrate on decorating the west wing.

Tracie stayed inside for the remainder of the day. She had hit a writer's block and had decided to watch some romantic comedies and take a nap. It was only in the past year or two that she had been able to watch those chick flicks again. After Nicholas had left, she just hadn't been able to watch the happily-ever-after stories. They were just a reminder of what she would never have.

But God had done a major healing in her life, and she was now able to watch them again—two or three in a row on some nights. She would do that when she had writer's block, hoping to get some thoughts or ideas for her book. The thing was, most of the time she gained plot ideas for future novels, not the one she was trying to complete. She had two other book ideas in the works but had not even finished her first one.

Tracie usually took a long weekend every month to come to the beach house. Over the past few years, Aunt Betty had encouraged her to come more often, telling her that the beach was good for the soul. For the past six weeks, she had been spending every weekend here. It was a quiet place to work on her book—a book that should have been completed by now.

Writing this book may not have been the best idea. It brought forth too many thoughts of what could have been but wasn't—and emotions she'd rather not deal with. Peggie, her counselor, had said she was a "stuffer." It was true. When you stuffed your emotions, you didn't have to deal with them, right? Not according to Peggie. She said, "You can only stuff so much before you explode. People have different ways of releasing those stuffed emotions—none of them good."

Peggie had actually encouraged Tracie to write the book to reflect her own story, knowing it would help bring to the surface all the feelings she needed to work through and allow God to heal. For Tracie, the feeling of rejection was the worst.

She didn't even like talking to Peggie about this. Peggie had a "feelings wheel," a color-coded circle labeled with different "feelings," and she would pull it out during their sessions. When they were in conversation about things that had happened, Peggie would always ask, "How does that make you feel?" Those deep conversations were always uncomfortable. Knowing that, Peggie would encourage her with the word of God and prayer before ending their session every week.

Ever since the day Nicholas had told her he was leaving, she'd felt empty, lost, and rejected. So, instead of writing a novel to reflect her past with all the hurt and disappointments, Tracie had opted to write a novel to reflect what she wanted her life to be, not what it was.

Chapter 3

*O*n Sunday morning, from the balcony of his beach house, Matthew let his gaze fall on the lady who was sitting in the blue-flowered chair again with her laptop. That beautiful black-and-white dog lay on a blanket beside her. Every weekend for the past six weeks he had seen her in that same spot, laptop in tow—though it seemed to him that she did more staring at the ocean than her laptop. Just as it had been every Saturday for the past six weeks, her medium-length hair, the color of espresso, was pulled into a ponytail and sticking out through the back opening of the Rays baseball cap she wore.

Matthew Carrington had basically been isolating himself after his wife's unexpected death seven years earlier. Now he was intrigued by the lady who has been coming to the beach every weekend. Should he step out of isolation and introduce himself to the mysterious lady on the beach?

He glanced down and saw the picture of Angela. *Aw, Angie, I miss you so much. The days are long, and the nights are lonely. It's been seven years.* He picked up the picture of himself and Angela, taken at the beach house the year before she'd been diagnosed with cancer. Her eyes were bright and blue. They twinkled like the stars. She had just had her hair cut into a bob that hit her just below her jaw line.

She had looked the picture of health, but within six months Matthew had laid her to rest.

They had just purchased the beach house in the spring after

Angie's father, Jim, had finally persuaded Matthew to take an early retirement. It had been their first trip to the beach house. Angie had brought her laptop along with her decorating program and had been at it for days, deciding how she wanted to decorate and ordering the furniture that would be delivered when they returned the following month.

Matthew had talked her into taking a break and going on a boat ride. He'd had the captain of the boat take their photo. He knew he needed to put that picture away. It was only keeping him from healing from the loss and moving forward.

Setting the photo back on the table, he heard that still, small voice again saying, "It is time, my son. 'For I know the plans I have for you, plans to prosper you and not to harm you, plans to give you a hope and a future (Jeremiah 29:11).'" That scripture verse had played over and over in Matthew's mind. He knew God's word to be true. He believed every word. Sometimes it was just hard to apply it to his life, to let it sink into his heart and head. He determined in his mind that today he would take a walk on the beach and introduce himself to the mystery lady.

"It's now or never," Matthew said to himself. "Get going before you lose your nerve." He put on a pair of khaki shorts and a light-blue T-shirt. Then he flipped the light off, slid into his flip-flops, and was out the door.

His heart rate escalated as he approached the beach chair where Tracie was sitting. *What is wrong with me?* he thought. *It's not like I'm a schoolboy getting ready to ask a girl to prom. I'm just going to say hello.* But instead of stopping, Matthew kept walking. He told himself that if he just took a little walk and a few deep breaths, it would be easier. He would just introduce himself on the way back. *What a coward!* he chided himself. As he continued to walk, he looked up and said, "God, I need a little help here. It's been far too long since I said more than hello to a lady in passing. I know I need to move forward and put your emotional healing in my life into action. Please, just give me the words to say."

Matthew headed back down the beach in the direction he had come, hoping the lady was still there and that he hadn't missed his opportunity. As he got closer, she came into view, still sitting there with her laptop open but staring at the ocean. At least he wouldn't be interrupting her work, only her thoughts. With that, he approached her and said hello.

"Um, I'm sorry, what was that?" the woman said. Matthew looked down at her and said hello again.

"Oh, hello." There was an awkward moment of silence before Matthew said, "I've noticed your visits to the beach for a long time now. I decided today to come and say hello." He pointed out his beach house just a little way up the beach to their right. He told her that he had noticed her in the same spot on weekends with her laptop and dog in tow. He reached out his hand to her and said, "My name is Matthew. Matthew Carrington. My family and my close friends call me Matthew. Everyone else just calls me Matt."

Tracie stood and took his hand in a light handshake. Smiling, she said, "Nice to meet you, Matt. I'm Tracie. Tracie Lawrence. My family and friends call me Tracie. Everyone else just calls me Tracie."

He let out a laugh. "Nice. Okay, I'll just call you Tracie. Do you live around here?"

After talking for a few minutes, Matthew asked her if she would like to go for a walk down the beach.

She said, "Sure, that would be great."

When they started walking he noticed that her dog stayed beside her instead of running out ahead as he'd seen the dog do at other times. *A good, loyal dog*, he thought, *watching out for her.*

They walked for about thirty minutes before Tracie said she needed to head back. Matthew was grateful for the opportunity to finally have met her and talked a little. Tracie shared that she was fulfilling a longtime dream of writing a novel in her spare time, when she wasn't decorating someone's home. Matthew told her he had retired to the beach and had taken up woodworking as a hobby.

When they got back to where Tracie's things were, she said, "It was nice meeting you, Matt. I enjoyed the walk and talk."

Matthew didn't want their meeting to end so quickly, but he didn't want to seem pushy either, so he said, "Maybe I'll see you next weekend."

Tracie said, "I'm sure you will. I'll probably be here every weekend until I finish my book."

Matthew asked if she would like to have dinner with him the following Saturday night. Then he said, "Maybe I'm being too forward, Tracie. I'm sorry."

"Oh, no, it's okay," Tracie said. "I just wasn't expecting to be asked to dinner. You see, I haven't dated at all since my divorce seven years ago."

Matt understood and told her he hadn't dated at all since his wife had passed away.

Tracie explained that her aunt was away this weekend but would be home the following Saturday. "Why don't you join Aunt Betty and me for dinner next Saturday?" she asked.

It was set. They parted ways with plans to meet next Saturday morning for a walk, and to have dinner with Aunt Betty at 6:00 p.m.

Chapter 4

As Tracie gathered up the few things she had brought with her and was heading out so as not to miss the ferry ride over to the parking area, her cell phone rang. She reached for it and looked at the caller ID. It was Nicholas.

Her heart did a quick flip-flop, but she did not answer the call. Nicholas hadn't said more than a cordial hello at family gatherings since he'd left seven years ago. He had never communicated well while they were married, and he'd done so rarely after leaving.

Thoughts of why he would call ran rampant through her mind. If it had been about Ella, their daughter, then Ella's husband, Jason, would have contacted her. Even if there had been an accident or something concerning Ella's daughter, Bailey, Tracie would have expected a call from anyone but Nicholas. After a minute she heard a familiar tone echo in the room. He had left a message.

Tracie didn't take time to listen to the message. If she missed that ferry, she would have to wait another two hours for the next one. She wanted to get home before it was late so she could concentrate on the busy work week ahead. She would listen to the message after she got in her car.

Tracie grabbed her overnight bag from the seat of the ferry and headed across the street where her car was parked in the secured lot. Once she was situated, with the car started and the air cooling it down, she pressed the button on her cell phone to listen to the message. It felt like a thousand butterflies had taken up residence in her belly. As she listened to the message, the feeling intensified. He wanted to talk to her, needed to talk to her. He said it was important. After seven years, what could he possibly have to say?

Tracie called Ella and asked how everyone was doing and if they'd had a nice weekend. Hearing that everyone was fine eased her mind somewhat, but the question of why Nicholas had to talk to her tormented her. She decided that she was not going to return his call.

Monday and Tuesday flew by. Tracie's business was growing rapidly. Having a home office was convenient, but today she was meeting with Mrs. Hoppinger, her newest client, to discuss ideas for her new living room furnishings.

Man, this lady was indecisive! First she wanted to go with a modern look, and then she thought maybe she would do a fashionable but eclectic look. Today she was saying that maybe a traditional look would best suit her. The lady was going to drive her to drink. It was Tuesday, five o'clock, and Tracie remembered she was supposed to meet Alice, her best friend, in the food court at the mall at six o'clock.

Tracie finally said, "Mrs. Hoppinger, I have another appointment in a half hour. I will put some layouts together with several options and get them to you next week."

"Well, what about tomorrow, dear?" Mrs. Hoppinger asked.

"I'm sorry, but I have a full schedule for the rest of the week. But I will leave these magazines with you to look through. Maybe it will help you decide which style you'd like to move ahead with. Is that all right?"

"Okay, dear. I'll wait to hear from you next week, then."

With that, Tracie was out the door before the client could think of another question that just couldn't wait.

There was no time to run home and take a nice, soothing shower. She and Alice had not been together for several weeks. She needed to talk to her about meeting Matthew at the beach and about the phone call from Nicholas. She had talked to Alice briefly about the call from Nicholas while driving home from the beach on Sunday, but Alice had only wanted the details of the "new beau," as she put it. Even though Tracie explained that they had only taken a walk on the beach and nothing more, Alice couldn't wait to have moment-by-moment details.

After a quick bite to eat and talking for nearly an hour, their conversation was interrupted with the ringing of Tracie's cell phone. "It's Nicholas again," Tracie said. "OMG, what in the world could he possibly want?"

Alice encouraged her to answer it, and her presence gave Tracie the courage to do so. She slid the button over and causally said, "Hello."

Only "hi" came from the other end of the line.

"Hi?" Tracie said. "You called just to say hi after seven years?"

"Tracie, I really need to talk to you," Nicholas responded. He was silent for a moment, which was normal conversational behavior for him. That much hadn't changed.

Tracie said, "I'm listening." She looked over at Alice, who was rolling her eyes.

Finally Nicholas said, "Can you meet me?"

"Meet you? Nicholas, what is up with you? You've said little more to me than hello when we're both at Ella's at the same time, and now you want to meet me somewhere? What will your wife think? I don't think she would be happy if you see me."

Silence. Alice's eyes weren't rolling now. Her big blue eyes where the size of saucers, and she scooted up to the edge of her seat.

Nicholas said, "Please, Tracie, I need to talk to you. It's important, and I don't want to say what I have to say over the phone."

Thoughts raced through Tracie's mind as she wondered what on earth Nicholas could have to say that was so important after all this time. "What do you have in mind?" she asked.

"I was hoping you would meet me for coffee after work on Friday. Thoughts of you flood my mind day and night. I've never told you how sorry I am for the way I left." His comments were shocking, to say the least. Tracie asked Nicholas to hold for a minute.

"Alice, he wants to meet me for coffee. Should I go, or should I decline? Oh, my word, I never expected this in a million years!" Tracie couldn't think straight.

Alice told her, "Hey, what do you have to lose? Go and see what he has to say. What about his wife? Is she going to come too?" Alice laughed.

Tracie went back to the line and asked Nicholas about Jessica. He said she was out of town and wouldn't be back until Sunday. Against her better judgment, Tracie ended the call after agreeing to meet him at 5:30 p.m. on Friday. As she was disconnecting the call, she looked at Alice and says, "I need my head examined to have agreed to this."

After that taxing conversation, Tracie was not in the mood to shop, but Alice dragged her to Macy's anyway, saying that they had a great sale.

When she finally got home that night, Tracie's mind was spinning. She went to the kitchen, opened the cabinet for a wine glass, pulled a bottle of Merlot out of the pantry, proceeded to the living room, and flopped onto the coach. She left the lights off.

"Oh, Lord, help me. I don't want to walk down that memory lane again. I need your peace, Lord. Maybe I should just call Nicholas back and tell him I can't meet with him."

You keep him in perfect peace whose mind is stayed on you, because he trusts in you. Trust in the Lord forever, for the Lord God is an everlasting rock (Isaiah 26:3–4 ESV).

Chapter 5

$\mathscr{M}$atthew sat in his beach house, anticipating the coming weekend. He was glad he'd finally gone down to the beach and met Tracie on Sunday morning, and he was looking forward to seeing her Saturday. He was trying to keep busy with a couple of do-it-yourself projects he had started in order to make the time pass more quickly. The days did seem to go by fast, but as the sun went down and he was inside the house, memories of Angela kept filling his thoughts.

The memories went all the way back to the day he had taken Angie as his bride. She had been beautiful in her simple white linen wedding gown. It was floor length and had tiny pearls sewn along the scoop neck. She'd worn white sandals, the straps being only strings of pearls. Her blonde hair had hung down almost to her waist. She hadn't wanted a fancy updo, though her maid of honor and best friend, Cindy, had wanted her to have one. Instead she had worn a crown of baby's breath with tiny pearls and white ribbons braided throughout, which had also hung down her back the same length as her hair.

The wedding had been simple, for Angela had not wanted a big wedding. She'd said it would be a waste of money that could be used toward other things, like decorating their first home. She did love interior design. She'd never gone to school for it but had taken online classes and watched lots of shows on the HGTV and DIY networks.

Everyone had thought that Matthew was too old for Angela, that he was robbing the cradle. He was forty and she was twenty-five.

As an only child, she had stood to inherit her father's business, and Matthew had been accused of marrying her for the family fortune.

Angela's father had not shared everyone else's opinion. Jim Anderson had known that Matthew loved his daughter. Not only had he been through long, heart-to-heart discussions with Matthew about Angela, but he'd recognized the look in Matthew's eyes every time Angela entered a room. He'd told Matthew that he had felt the same way when he looked at his own lovely wife, Sandra. He'd claimed that Sandra was beyond beautiful, even as she got older. Her auburn hair had fallen around her shoulders, glistening like the morning dew on autumn leaves. Her green eyes had had a twinkle in them that had sent his heart racing. Matthew had never had the pleasure of meeting Sandra, as she had passed away about two years before he'd met the Andersons.

Matthew and Angela had been married for fifteen years when she lost the battle to cancer at the age of forty. Seven years had gone by since that sad day. Jim had suffered a massive heart attack, which took his life just six months after Angie's death. Angie had never been able to have children, so now Matthew was pretty much alone.

Not liking where his thoughts were going, Matthew picked up his Bible, opened it to Psalm 121, and began reading.

I lift up my eyes to the hills. Where does my help come from? My help comes from the Lord, the maker of heaven and earth.

He will not let your foot slip. He who watches over you will not slumber. Indeed, he who watches over Israel will neither slumber or sleep.

The Lord watches over you. The Lord is your shade at your right hand; the sun will not harm you by day, nor the moon by night.

The Lord will keep you from all harm. He will watch over your life. The Lord will watch over your coming and going, both now and forevermore.

Reading the book of Psalms always seemed to soothe Matthew. He prayed, thanking God for watching over him and asking him to direct his steps.

Chapter 6

$\mathcal{N}$icholas O'Conner had thought the grass was greener on the other side of the fence, so after twenty years of marriage to his high school sweetheart, he had divorced her. Within only a few months, he had married Jessica. Not long after remarrying, he'd realized that it had been a grave mistake. After living that mistake for seven years, Nicholas had decided he couldn't continue living as if everything was as great as he'd dreamed it would be.

He'd heard that Tracie hadn't dated anyone else since he'd left. Why should that surprise him? He'd known that she didn't want the divorce. He remembered the last thing she'd said to him before he left: "I will go to my grave loving you." But that was a long time ago, and even if she wasn't dating anyone, should he be so brazen to think that she would give him another chance? He hadn't told Tracie that he and Jessica were separated, that they had already begun the divorce process. He didn't want to scare her away. He only wanted to talk to her, to apologize and see where it might lead.

Tracie's head was spinning as she waited for Nicholas outside Starbucks. She had already gone inside and ordered her coffee— nothing fancy, just black coffee. Her stomach was in knots, because she had no clue why he suddenly wanted to talk to her. It was only 5:20 p.m., so he wasn't late, but she just wanted this night to be over. Why in heaven's name had she ever agreed to this?

Tracie had gone to one of the outside tables and was sipping her coffee when she saw the black Corvette pull into the parking lot. Her heart rate increased, and her palms starting sweating. "Lord, please calm my racing heart," she prayed quietly. Nicholas stepped out of his car and walked to the table where she was sitting. He started to ask her if she wanted anything, and she pointed to her cup. He said he would be right back and went inside to order his coffee.

While Nicholas was gone, Tracie prayed silently that God would give her the words to say to him, even though she had no idea what he was going to talk about. Then she saw him heading out the door and back to her table. Why did he have to look so good? This would be a lot easier if the sight of him didn't still stir her heart.

Taking the chair across from her, Nicholas said, "Thanks for agreeing to meet me."

"Um, sure. What's on your mind?"

"Tracie, I know I should have asked for your forgiveness a long time ago, but I never found a time that seemed right."

"Nicholas, really, I—"

"Tracie, please, let me finish," he said.

She nodded, and he continued.

"This isn't easy for me, so I just want to say what I need to say, okay?"

"Sure," Tracie said, even as she thought, *Yeah, just say whatever it is you have to say, and we can be done with this uncomfortable meeting.*

"I only thought of myself when I left. I wasn't thinking of you or your feelings. I wasn't considering the impact my leaving would have on Ella or Bailey. After Jessica and I were married, I never had the opportunity to apologize. I want you to know how sorry I am for all the pain I caused you." Nicholas picked up his coffee and took a sip.

Tracie just sat there, staring at him. Finally she said, "Why now, Nicholas?"

"Jessica and I are separated," he said. "Actually, I've already filed for divorce."

"Oh, so now that Jessica is not controlling your every move, you can apologize. Is that it?"

"Yes. No. I mean, I'm not apologizing just because Jessica and I are getting a divorce," Nicholas tried to explain. "I realized a few years ago that I had made a terrible decision to leave you. I guess I was having a midlife crisis or something. After that, I didn't know how to undo what I'd done."

"You could have just walked out on her like you walked out on me," Tracie said. "It seems like it should be easier to leave someone you've only been with a few years rather than someone with whom you spent almost half your life."

Nicholas sat there for a few minutes without saying a word. He took another sip of his coffee, sat back from the table, and said, "This is more difficult than I anticipated." He smiled a half smile.

"Does Ella know you and Jessica are getting a divorce"? Tracie asked.

"Not yet. I haven't brought the subject up."

"So, you're going to wait until after the fact to tell Ella, like you did when you got remarried?"

Nicholas remained silent.

Tracie backtracked. "That wasn't right for me to say, Nicholas. I just know how hurt Ella was when you first left and didn't share anything with her. I don't know if she's ever talked to you about how difficult those first couple of years were for her and Bailey. It was hard for her to watch me going through the emotional pain while working through her own feelings as well."

They sat there for several minutes, neither of them saying a word. Then Tracie said, "Nicholas, I know this wasn't easy for you. I've thought for a couple of years now that I should let you know I've forgiven you for leaving. I forgive you for the emotional trauma I went through. It was not easy. It took me years of counseling and a lot of prayers from my family and friends to get me through. God has healed me emotionally, and I'm at a good place in my life now. I have a successful business of my own, and I've finally started writing the novel I've always wanted to write."

Nicholas didn't say anything. He just sat there looking at his coffee cup. Then he said, "Tracie, can we have dinner tomorrow night? There's still a lot I want to say to you, but I'm having a difficult time expressing myself tonight."

"I'm sorry, Nicholas. I'm going to Aunt Betty's for the weekend. I've been spending quite a bit of time on the island these past few months."

"Oh, okay," Nicholas said. "Well, can I call you next week?"

"I don't know, Nicholas. This is really weird. I don't know how I feel about going to dinner with you. I mean, I wasn't even sure about meeting you tonight. After all, you're still a married man, and to me, that matters." Tracie went on. "Nicholas, think about talking to Ella. I know she will be there for you during this time. She is so sweet, Nicholas. She's someone you can talk to and know she will be there for you if you need anything." Trace got to her feet. "It's been a long day. I have to get up early in the morning and head to Aunt Betty's."

As she gathered her purse and keys, Nicholas stood and said, "Thanks again for meeting me. Hope you have a nice weekend."

Tracie nodded. As she drove away in her car, she saw him watching her.

Just as Tracie was pulling into her driveway, Alice called. When Tracie picked up the phone, she said, "I thought I was supposed to call you." She laughed as she said it.

"I couldn't stand it any longer. Spill it! What did Nicholas want?"

"Are you sitting down?" Tracie asked.

"That good, huh?" Alice said. "He and Jessica must be splitting up."

"Wow. Why would you say that?" Tracie asked.

"Well, if they were together, she wouldn't have let him go to meet you for coffee." She laughed as she spoke. "Besides, everyone knew that marriage would never last. So, am I right? Is it true?"

"Yes. He's filed for divorce, and he wanted to apologize to me for leaving and for putting me through all the emotional pain his leaving caused me. He wanted to have dinner with me tomorrow night."

"Seriously?" Alice sounded like she couldn't believe it.

"I know, right?" Tracie said. "I told him I was going to Aunt Betty's for the weekend."

"Did you also tell him you have a hot date tomorrow night?" Alice asked, laughing.

"Alice! I do not have a hot date!"

"Sure you do. You're having dinner with Matthew, right?"

"And Aunt Betty," Tracie said defensively. "Alice, I don't even know this guy, so I would hardly call it a hot date. More like dinner with a neighbor."

"A neighbor?" Alice asked.

"Yes, he's Aunt Betty's neighbor."

"Okay, if you say so," Alice said. "Listen, I'll let you go. Call me when you head home on Sunday."

With that, the phone conversation ended. Tracie was ready to take a nice long bubble bath and relax with a glass of wine.

Chapter 7

*I*t was warm when Tracie headed south on I-75 toward Gasparilla Island on Saturday morning. September was usually quite warm, with highs still reaching into the low nineties. There was always a nice breeze on the beach, so Tracie didn't mind the warmth. Besides, her tan from beaching it all summer would fade soon if the winter weather was as cool as had been predicted for this year.

Tracie was grateful that Aunt Betty had brunch on the table when she walked in. She had gone through McDonald's drive-through for coffee on her way, but now her tummy was letting her know of its neglect. She could smell Aunt Betty's prized blueberry muffins before she opened the front door. There was also a big bowl of fruit with fresh cantaloupe, blueberries, strawberries, raspberries, pineapple, and bananas. Vanilla yogurt and homemade granola topped off the brunch.

"Aunt Betty, you've really outdone yourself," Tracie told her with a kiss on the cheek.

"Oh, Tracie, I just threw some fruit in and bowl and made some muffins," Aunt Betty responded. "It's nothing fancy."

"Well, my stomach thanks you," Tracie said. "I'm half starved."

Aunt Betty asked Tracie to say grace. She prayed a simple blessing for the food and thanked the Lord for her aunt's safe return home.

As they ate, Tracie asked her aunt about her trip.

Aunt Betty said the weather had already started to dip into the low forties at night. The days were nice, though, with highs in the upper sixties to low seventies.

"How is Uncle Tom?" Tracie asked.

"I'm a little concerned about him," Aunt Betty said. "He's getting so feeble, Tracie, but I can't seem to talk him into assisted living. He says, 'I've live in this old house for sixty-five years, and I'll stay here until I meet my maker.' He's as stubborn as an old goat."

Tracie chuckled at the comment, because Aunt Betty had been known to have a stubborn streak as well.

"Your dad drove in for a couple of days," Aunt Betty added. "We had a good time. The three of us reminisced about the good ole days."

"Aw, that's nice," Tracie said. "How's my dad? I talk to him once a week, but you know him—a man of few words."

"He seems to be doing well. Says he spends his days in the barn and working on his garden."

Tracie's dad had moved to North Carolina after retiring thirteen years ago. He'd always been pretty much a loner, but he seemed to be happy, so that was all that mattered to Tracie.

"I met one of our neighbors last Saturday while I was on the beach," Tracie told her aunt. "His name is Matt. He's been on the island for several years, but normally he keeps to himself."

"That's nice, dear. It's good that you're meeting some of the neighbors." Aunt Betty looked carefully at her. "You look like you haven't been sleeping well, girl. What's troubling you?"

As Tracie continued to nibble on her muffin, she shared with Aunt Betty about the meeting with Nicholas. She told her aunt that she was freaked out by the fact that he and Jessica were getting a divorce. She told her aunt she'd dreamed about being with him again and had tossed and turned for most the night. She'd finally gotten up at about 4:00 a.m. and begun writing the next chapter in her book, trying to get her mind off Nicholas.

Aunt Betty said, "That explains those dark circles under those beautiful green eyes."

"Ugh! Seriously? I bet I'm a mess," Tracie said. "Did I tell you I'm supposed to walk the beach with Matthew this morning? I don't know why I agreed to meet him this morning, and for dinner—oh my word, Aunt Betty, what was I thinking? He's supposed to have dinner with us too!"

"Tracie, dear, you need to calm down. Why are you worrying? God has all of this under control. Let me share a devotional I read just yesterday. It's from *Jesus Calling* by Sarah Young." Aunt Betty rose to get her book. When she returned, she began reading aloud.

"Bring me your weakness, and receive My peace. Accept yourself and your circumstances just as they are, remembering that I am sovereign over everything. Do not wear yourself out with analyzing and planning. Instead, let thankfulness and trust be your guides through this day;

they will keep you close to Me. As you live in the radiance of My Presence, My Peace shines upon you. You will cease to notice how weak or strong you feel, because you will be focusing on Me. The best way to get through this day is step by step with Me. Continue this intimate journey, trusting that the path you are following is headed for heaven.

"'The Lord gives strength to his people; the Lord blesses his people with peace' (Psalm 29:11)."

Tracie sat quietly for a few minutes until Aunt Betty said, "Go on down to the beach and take your walk, Tracie. I have tonight's dinner all planned out, so just relax."

Tracie thanked her for her encouragement. She looked at Max and said, "You want to go to the beach, boy?" Max was up and at the door before she could turn around.

"I should be back in about an hour, Aunt Betty," Tracie called over her shoulder as she headed toward the door.

"Take your time, dear—and wear your sunglasses," she said with a chuckle.

"Very funny, Aunt Betty. You do know that I'm not trying to impress Matt, right? I'm just being nice and neighborly."

Tracie pushed her sunglasses up onto her nose as she headed to the front door.

Chapter 8

Matthew was sitting on the beach very near Tracie's usual spot when she and Max approached him. "Good morning," he called to her as he reached out to scratch Max's ears.

"Good morning," Tracie replied.

"How was your week?" Matthew asked.

"Let's just say that I'm glad the weekend is here."

"That good, huh?" Matthew said, rising to his feet.

"I'm sure a walk on the beach will help," Tracie said. "It usually does."

Matthew appeared to be much more relaxed today than he'd been when he'd first introduced himself last weekend. Tracie wished she could say the same for herself. Although she appeared relaxed to those around her, there was a war raging within her heart and mind.

She tried to clear her mind of the strange conversation she'd had with Nicholas the night before, hoping against hope that he would not call her this weekend. Matthew seemed like a really nice guy, and she wanted to spend the weekend getting to know him a little better. It had been a long time since she'd had any male companionship, even a "just friends" relationship.

As they began walking, Max just sat there. Tracie looked back at him and said, "Come on, boy, or are you just going to sit there and wait for me to get back?" Max cocked his head to one side and looked at her with those big brown eyes. "Come on, Max. Let's go chase the waves." With that, he was up and running. He ran right up to the shore as a wave was going back out. When another wave broke and washed quickly on shore, Max backed up, barking at it and turning in circles. Then he followed it as it washed back out again.

Matthew seemed to be enjoying the playful banter between Tracie and her dog. "Seeing Max makes me think about adopting a dog from the shelter in town," he said. "It would be nice to have the companionship."

"Max really is a great companion," Tracie agreed as they walked. "How has your week been?"

Matthew said he'd had a pretty good week. He had taken some long walks on the beach, looking for driftwood.

"What are you doing with the driftwood you find?" Tracie asked.

"I'm making a couple of small tables for my deck. I'm keeping a beach theme up there. I figured the driftwood will hold up well against the weather."

Tracie was intrigued. "So, you are a craftsman? A builder? A carpenter?"

Matthew laughed. "None of the above, really. I've just started tinkering with some woodworking and such over the past few years. Keeps me sane. I retired about six months before my wife passed away. I try to find things to fill my days."

"I'm sorry for your loss," Tracie said. "How long were you married?"

"We were married fifteen years," Matthew said. "Angie, my wife, was only forty when she lost the battle with cancer. She was only twenty-five when we were married. I was forty. I'd worked with her father for several years, and I met her at a company Christmas party. It was love at first sight. Everyone thought I just wanted to marry her for the family fortune, but I truly loved her. Lucky for me, her father believed me and allowed me to court her for a year. Then he gave his blessing for us to marry."

"That is so sweet," Tracie said.

"Okay, enough about me," Matthew said. "Tell me about you."

"Oh, gee, where do I start?" Tracie asked, adjusting her ball cap and sunglasses.

"Well, I don't see a ring on your finger, so you must be single."

"I was married for twenty years to my high school sweetheart," she replied.

"Did he pass away?" Matthew asked.

"Not exactly."

Matthew didn't say anything further, so she continued. "He left me for a younger woman. Midlife crisis, I guess."

"I'm so sorry, Tracie. I can't imagine how difficult that must have been."

"It has taken me a long time to get my life back on course," Trace said. "I've used Aunt Betty's beach house as a refuge. It's been very therapeutic for me." Since she was wearing sunglasses, she was able to hide her emotions as she shared the part of her life that had been less than pleasant.

"The years have been difficult for me since Angela's passing," Matthew said, "but she didn't leave me by choice. I can take comfort in that." He hesitated. "Tracie, you must be a very strong person. Can I ask you a personal question?"

"Sure," she replied. "We're bearing our hearts here anyway, right?"

"Are you a Christian?" he asked.

"Yes. Yes, I am," she said. "My relationship with God is what got me through the past seven years. It was His strength, not mine—that and the love of family and friends. I read the psalms a lot and pray. Psalm 28:7 says, 'The Lord is my strength and my shield; my heart trusts in Him and I am helped.'"

"I'm a Christian too," Matthew said. "I also read the psalms a lot. It's like a soothing balm for the soul."

Chapter 9

"The evening is going to be much too nice to eat inside," Aunt Betty said. "The weatherman predicted that tonight's low should drop down to about seventy-two degrees as a cold front comes through. We shall dine on the patio off the kitchen. Is that okay with you, dear?"

"That sounds wonderful," Tracie said. "What can I do to help?"

"Everything is pretty much ready to go. The steaks are marinating, and the salad is all put together and in the fridge. The potatoes are washed and wrapped. The asparagus has been washed, cut, seasoned, and wrapped in foil, ready to throw on the grill with the steaks. Garlic toast is in the freezer. It's store bought, but it's the best. I like it."

"Wow, you have been busy," Tracie said. "I was gone for less than two hours, and you accomplished a lot. I'll make dessert, then. How's that?"

"I already did. I just whipped up that chocolate raspberry mousse you like so well. It's full of flavor and will be nice and light after our big meal."

Aunt Betty had made up some egg salad and had sandwiches waiting on the table along with freshly squeezed lemonade. They enjoyed the light lunch, and then Aunt Betty sent Tracie to the "west wing" to rest, work on her book, primp, or do whatever for the rest of the afternoon.

It was one o'clock, and Matthew wouldn't be arriving for another five hours. Tracie decided to try to finish the chapter of her book she'd started last night when she couldn't sleep. It wouldn't take more than an hour or so. Then she would rest for a couple of hours, which would still leave plenty of time for a shower before six o'clock.

Tracie woke with a start to Aunt Betty's tapping on her door. She found herself lying in her big, comfy leather recliner with her notes fallen to the floor and scattered all around. Her pen was teetering on the edge of the chair's arm. It was already 4:30. She groaned and thanked her aunt for waking her. Who knew how long she would have dozed otherwise? She hurried to get ready for dinner.

Tracie had just finished applying her deep-rose lip gloss, when she heard the doorbell chime. She whispered a quick prayer for a nice evening and went down to greet her guest.

Matthew's eyes lit up when she opened the door, and he smiled. She knew he had never seen her without her hair pulled through the back of a baseball cap. She wore a rose-colored dress with a thin black belt and black sandals. She had applied brown eye shadow with a touch of emerald eyeliner to bring out her green eyes.

Matthew was a very attractive man with short, stylish gray hair and the most amazing blue eyes Tracie had ever seen. They were the color of the deep-blue ocean. His choice of attire was a nice collared golf shirt in a pale blue, khaki shorts, and brown leather flip-flops. *Perfect for backyard dining at the beach*, she thought. Tracie and Matthew chatted for a few minutes and then headed to the kitchen to see if Aunt Betty needed some help.

"Tracie, ask what our guest would like to drink," Aunt Betty said. "I'll have iced tea. If you make the drinks and head out to the patio, I'll join you shortly. And Matthew, would you be so kind as to fire up the grill for me?"

"Sure, ma'am, I can do that," he replied.

"Please, call me Betty. *Ma'am* sounds like you're talking to my mother."

Tracie was grateful that Aunt Betty had used the phrase "our guest." It made this seem less like a date and more like dinner with a new friend—which was what it was, really, wasn't it?

Tracie got their drinks—iced tea for Aunt Betty, freshly squeezed lemonade for Matthew, and a glass of water for herself—and then headed to the patio with Matthew following.

Aunt Betty had outdone herself. The patio table was set up with her simple white Corelle dinnerware upon an ocean-blue tablecloth. The centerpiece was one of Tracie's favorites: a double glass vase that held a blue-and-white three-wick candle. The outer vase was full of the rocks and shells Tracie had picked up on the beach the day she'd had the revelation about what people had in common with rocks and shells. Tracie would have to mention to her aunt how special that was.

Matthew offered to grill the steaks, and Aunt Betty readily accepted the kind offer. It was nice, because all three of them liked their steaks medium well. They were cooked to perfection, as was the rest of the meal.

Conversation was light and cheery while they were eating.

"How long how you lived on the island?" Aunt Berry asked.

"Almost eight years," Matthew replied.

"What brought you here?" Betty continued. "Do you have other family here?"

"No, no other family here. The year before I retired, my wife and I purchased the property. She had lots of plans for decorating our place and moving here, but I lost her to cancer several months after we purchased the property. I almost sold the beach house when Angie passed, but her father encouraged me to continue on with our plans.

When they were finished with their meal, they sat there chatting for another twenty minutes. As Aunt Betty rose to clear the table, Tracie and Matthew both got up to help. Aunt Betty insisted that they stay and enjoy the nice evening while she made coffee and got the dessert.

After Aunt Betty left for the kitchen, Matthew looked at Tracie. She could feel the color rising to her cheeks when she realized he was watching her. He said, "You know, this is the first time I've seen you without your sunglasses and that baseball cap you wear. You are a very pretty lady."

The color in her cheeks deepened. She did not receive compliments well. She did not know how to respond, so she simply said thank you.

Matthew said, "I haven't spent a lot of time with you, Tracie, but you seem to be as beautiful on the inside as you are on the outside."

"Aw, that is so sweet," she responded. "Thank you, Matt."

Aunt Betty's arrival with dessert and coffee could not have been more timely, because Tracie didn't know what else to say to Matt at the moment.

After dessert and coffee, they moved into the living room. Aunt Betty always referred to it as the "sitting" room. She always said, "After all, dear, we *sit* in here; we do not *live* in here." Matt took a seat at one end of the love seat facing two recliners. Aunt Betty sat in one recliner, and Tracie sat in the other one across from Matt.

Aunt Betty began the conversation by asking Matt if he had ever attended the little church on the island. He said he used to go there until a few years ago when they quit having regular services. "Well," Aunt Betty said, "I hear they're having a contemporary worship service tomorrow morning at ten, if you'd like to join Tracie and me."

"That's very kind of you, Betty. I think I will—if it's okay with Tracie.

"Of course, that's fine, Matt," Tracie replied, playing with the fringe on the throw lying on the arm of her chair.

Matthew headed home about 8:00 p.m. It was just beginning to get dark. After the door closed behind him, Aunt Betty yawned and said, "I think I'll head to the east wing for the night."

Tracie stopped her in her tracks and said, "Oh, no you don't, lady!"

"What do you mean?" Aunt Betty asked, smiling. "Is something wrong?"

"Are you trying to get Matt and me together by inviting him to church with us tomorrow?" Tracie asked.

"Why, no, dear," her aunt said, raising her eyebrows in that teasing way she did when she was up to something. I just thought it would be a nice gesture to invite our new friend to church."

"I do have a novel to complete," Tracie reminded her aunt.

"Far be it from me to come between a girl and her novel," said Aunt Betty, giving a little wink. "But a girl does need to have breaks from time to time, you know. All work and no play will make for a boring story. Besides, you should not miss church when you have the opportunity to go."

"Aunt Betty, you are deplorable, but I love you," Tracie said. "Now, off to the east wing you go." She gave her aunt a hug.

Tracie made her way to her the west wing and sat down in her big, comfy chair. She put pen to paper, and before she knew it, the clock had struck midnight. She had just finished chapter 12. Tracie felt that she had accomplished a lot. Her book was about half complete now. She was ready for a good night's sleep.

Chapter 10

$\mathcal{T}$racie was grateful she hadn't heard from Nicholas since they'd met at Starbucks last Friday night, but she knew her luck was about to run out. Tonight was her granddaughter, Bailey's, birthday—and her reason for not being at the beach house this weekend. She knew Nicholas would probably be there.

Tracie didn't want to think about Nicholas right now. Her mind drifted back to last Saturday night when she's gotten her first good look at Matthew without his sunglasses. He was a very attractive man. He looked amazing for his sixty-two years. He was buff and tan, and his eyes were as blue as the ocean. There was a definite twinkle in them when he laughed or smiled. "I don't know why I'm letting my mind take this direction," Tracie said out loud, even though there was no one else in her living room.

"Friends, just friends, and weekend neighbors. That is all." Tracie reminded herself.

As she got ready for Bailey's party, her phone rang. She froze. "Oh, Lord, please, don't let it be Nicholas," she said, grabbing the phone off the coffee table. She was relieved when she saw Ella's sweet face on the screen staring back at her.

"Ella, how are you?" Tracie said. "Got everything ready for tonight"?

"Hello to you too, Mom," Ella said, laughing.

"Sorry, I was distracted when the phone rang," Tracie said.

"Oh, do you have company?" Ella asked.

"No, why?" Tracie said.

"I don't know. You just sound different."

"I have a lot on my mind, that's all. Have you talked to your dad?"

"No, why?" Ella asked.

"Oh, I just wondered if he was going to be at Bailey's party, that's all," she responded.

"I invited them, but I haven't heard for sure if they're coming. Oh, hold on a minute, Mom, it's Dad calling now. Don't hang up. I'll make it quick with Dad."

After several seconds, Ella's voice came through the phone again. "Mom, are you there?"

"Yes, I'm here," Tracie said. "Everything okay?"

"Yeah. Dad just said he would be here tonight, but Jessica isn't coming."

"Really? That's strange, don't you think? She never lets him go anywhere by himself." Tracie's tone was not so nice.

"Mom!" Ella said in a sharper than usual tone.

"I'm sorry," Tracie said. "I know it's not my business. Anyway, you didn't call to talk about this, sweet girl. What's up?"

"I just wanted to make sure you remembered that you were going to pick up the cake for me," Ella replied.

"Yep. Sam's on Fruitville Road, right?" Tracie clarified.

"Yes."

"Okay, little girl. I'll see you in a couple of hours. You're sure you don't need anything else?"

"No, we're good. Jason is going to start the grill about five o'clock. The burgers won't take that long to cook. Bailey wants to swim some first. Everyone will be arriving about four o'clock.

Bailey's party was a large gathering. Kids only became a teenager once. All of Bailey's friends from church were there, and most of their parents as well. Everyone had brought a dish, chips, or drinks to share. That made it nice for Ella and Jason, as parties could be very costly.

Nicholas didn't have much to say all evening, which Tracie thought weird, but she was grateful. Then again, she had avoided him as much as possible. She had just given Bailey a hug, said her goodbyes, and headed for the door, when she heard Nicholas call her name.

She stopped and looked around. He was the only one in the room with her.

"Nicholas, um, hey," she stammered.

"I was wondering if we could have dinner one night this week," he said as he was approaching her.

"I'm not at all comfortable going to dinner with you while you're still married," she replied, "especially since no one seems to know that you and Jessica are even separated."

"I know," he said. "I'm staying after Bailey's party to talk to Ella. I'm going to tell her everything. I filed the divorce papers yesterday. Jessica has twenty-one days to contest. If things go as I think they will, she is not going to fight this. The divorce should be final soon after that—well, as soon as we can get a court date."

"The courts sure work quickly," she said. "Sad that it doesn't even give people a chance to change their minds, does it?"

"I'm not going to change my mind, Tracie," Nicholas responded. "I should have acted on this a long time ago."

"Listen, Nicholas, I really need to go. I have to work on some plans for a job I have on Monday, and I don't have much done yet." Tracie inched her way to the door as she spoke.

"If you won't go to dinner with me, Tracie, can I at least call you?" he pleaded.

"Um, I don't know. I—I guess so." And with that she walked out the door before he could pressure her further.

Nicholas wasted no time in calling her. No sooner had she returned home from her client's house on Monday evening before her phone rang. She started to let it go to voice mail, but when she saw Nicholas's number, she decided to take the call and get it over with.

"Hello," she answered.

"Tracie, this is Nicholas. Is this a good time to for you to talk?"

"Good as any, I suppose," she said.

"I know this is weird for you," he continued. "It's weird for me too."

"Well, it is awkward. Most conversations we've had for the past seven or eight years have been cordial at best—for the sake of Ella and Bailey."

"Speaking of Ella, I talked to her and Jason Saturday night after the party," Nicholas said.

"What did they have to say about you divorcing Jessica?" Tracie asked.

"Jason has never like Jessica," Nicholas said. "He was always friendly enough to her, but I knew he never wanted us together, Tracie. He has been more like a son than a son-in-law. He even came to my office on the day of our divorce before I went to court and tried to talk me out of going through with it. He said that God hated divorce and that I still had time to change my mind. I should have listened to him then."

"What about Ella?" Tracie asked.

"She's the peacemaker. She wanted to make sure I knew what I was doing. She didn't seem happy or sad. She did say she hoped she would see me more often now, and she told me she would always be there for me if I needed anything. You've done a great job with our daughter, Tracie. She is a very mature and responsible adult. She also seems to have a great relationship with the Lord, which is more than I can say about myself."

Tracie knew Ella would try to witness to her dad. She always did, even when it went in one ear and out the other. "That's probably the first thing you need to work on, Nicholas," she said.

"What?" he asked.

"Taking steps to get your relationship right with God. Long

before you walked away from me, Nicholas, you walked away from him. You need to get involved in a church somewhere and surrender control of your life to God again. That would be your first step to finding true happiness." Tracie wondered if this would be the end of their conversation.

"Would you mind if I started going back to The Tabernacle?" he asked.

"This is a decision you need to make from your heart—for you and only you. Talk to your sister. You know Diane is attending The Tabernacle now. Maybe you can go with her. I'm sure she would love to restore her relationship with you too. She misses you. She told me you slowly drifted away from her and the rest of family after our divorce."

"What about you, Tracie? Do you miss me?"

"Listen, Nicholas, I think it's time to say good night," Tracie responded. "I'm glad you talked to Ella and Jason and aren't keeping them in the dark with what's happening in your life. I'm sure it means a lot to them. I need to go now."

"I'll be in touch, Tracie," he said. "Have a nice evening."

And with that, Tracie disconnected the call. She could not believe that Nicholas had had the nerve to ask if she missed him. At times she *had* missed him, missed him so much she hadn't thought she would survive. But for the past two years, she had successfully put aside her thoughts and feelings for him. Even though she hadn't dated anyone since the divorce, she hadn't spent her thoughts on him anymore, either.

Now there was the prospect of Matt. It was far too early in their friendship to know if an actual relationship might blossom, but she sure would consider it. What little she knew about Matthew Carrington, she liked.

Chapter 11

*A*fter two long weeks at home, Tracie was ready to go to the beach house. She had hoped to make it down for the 10:00 a.m. ferry to Little Gasparilla, but she had failed to set her alarm. She hadn't thought it necessary because she was almost always awake by 6:00 a.m., even on weekends. Her sleep lately had been restless and full of dreams she wished she didn't have. But last night had been different. She'd slept like a rock, not even getting up in the middle of the night to use the restroom.

When she woke up, the sun was shining bright. To her amazement, the bedside clock read 9:08 a.m. She would have time for coffee and a shower and could still make the noon crossing to the island. She would call Aunt Betty to ask if she needed anything from the store on her way and to let her know she would not be there until after 12:30 p.m. instead of her normal arrival at 10:30 a.m.

This morning she was grateful for the Keurig single-cup coffee maker Ella and Jason had given her for Christmas the year before last. She needed coffee this morning and didn't want to wait for a pot to brew.

Coffee in hand, she moved to the breakfast nook where she'd left her phone last night.

Taking a long drink of coffee, she picked up the phone and dialed Aunt Betty's number. After the third ring, her aunt answered and said, "I'm glad you called, Tracie. Do you think you have time to stop by the market and pick up some fresh broccoli and still make the ten o'clock ferry?"

"Well, good morning to you too, Aunt Betty," Tracie said.

"Oh, sorry, dear, I was focused on asking you to stop at Publix before you pass it on the way to meet the ferry," Aunt Betty responded.

"I can stop for you, Aunt Betty, but I won't be making the early ferry. That's why I'm calling."

"Is everything all right? Are you okay, dear?" Aunt Betty sounded concerned.

Tracie explained that she had overslept and had not left the house yet. She told her aunt that she would stop by the store. If her aunt thought of anything else she needed, she could call back.

Once on the road, Tracie's mind replayed the past week. Monday had been the awkward phone call from Nicholas. It was strange that he hadn't tried to call again during the week. She was glad he hadn't, but she'd thought he would have. "I hope he doesn't call while I'm at the beach house," she said to herself. "That's my place of refuge, and I don't want to deal with him this weekend."

Then there had been the indecisive Mrs. Hoppinger, who was getting on her last nerve. The woman had narrowed down her selection to modern or eclectic, taking traditional off the list. Tracie had left her a layout of modern, sleek, clean lines, along with another plan with mismatched but stylish choices. Mrs. Hoppinger had promised to have a decision for Tracie on Tuesday.

Her mind continued racing through the rest of the week. She had picked up two new clients. One sweet widow lady, Mrs. Jones— who insisted on being called May Belle—only wanted to "freshen up" her sitting room. Then there was Bob. Actually, he was her first male client and a bachelor. Bob said that a colleague at work had given him her number. His colleague had a friend who knew Rosie, someone Tracie had done some decorating for last year. Word of mouth was the best advertisement, Tracie thought.

The phone rang, jolting her out of the week in review. She glanced down at the phone, saw Aunt Betty's precious face staring back at her, clicked her Bluetooth earpiece, and said, "Hey, Aunt Betty"—just as she was pulling into the Publix parking lot.

"Tracie, I thought of a couple more things I need from the market," her aunt said.

"You have perfect timing, Aunt Betty. I just pulled in front of the Publix."

"Good. I need you to get three nice-size chicken breasts and some spinach linguini. I want to make that 'chicken pizzarella' you like so well for our noon meal tomorrow."

"Don't we need only two chicken breasts?" Tracie asked.

"I thought it would be nice if we asked Matthew to join us," her aunt replied.

"Aren't you being a little presumptuous?" Tracie asked.

"If he doesn't want to join us, I'll have leftovers next week, which is fine, since I don't make this recipe very often." Her aunt rattled on. "Somehow I don't think Matthew will turn down an invitation for a home-cooked meal. You know, on second thought, go ahead and get *four* nice-size chicken breasts. I'll plan on having leftovers one day."

"All right, let me go so I don't miss the twelve o'clock ferry. I'll see you soon, Aunt Betty," Tracie said and ended the call.

Tracie looked at Max lying in the back seat. "I'll be right back, boy." He lifted his head to look at her and then laid it back down.

Just as Tracie was stepping off the ferry, her phone rang again. With her hands full, she didn't dig for the phone to see who was calling. She just pushed the Bluetooth button and said hello.

"Hello, Tracie." The sound of Nicholas's voice came through the phone. *Oh, great,* Tracie thought, rolling her eyes. *He has the lousiest timing.*

"Hey, Nicholas."

"Are you busy? Is this a good time to talk?" he asked.

"No, I'm sorry, Nicholas, this is not a good time to talk. I just stepped off the ferry on the island. I stopped by the store on the way, and I have Max in tow, so I really need to go. I'll call you back in a couple of hours once I get settled, if that's okay."

"Sure, I'll be home all day, so when you get time, just call. Thanks, Tracie. I look forward to your call."

A soon as Tracie hung up, she asked herself, "Why in the world did I tell him I'd call him back later? I don't want to call him back while I'm at Aunt Betty's. This beach house is my refuge. I don't want to share the time I have here with Nicholas, even if it's just a phone call."

Aunt Betty met Tracie at the door and relieved her of part of the load she was carrying. Tracie had picked up a few more things from the store than her aunt had requested. "Junk food," as her aunt called it, was what she was in the mood for—a junk-food weekend. When Tracie had passed the chips aisle, she'd grabbed a big bag of Ruffles, and then, of course, she needed pimento cheese to dip them in. The onion dip had just about jumped off the shelf and into her basket by itself. On the way to the checkout line, she'd passed a cookie display featuring Pinwheels, and she'd grabbed those too. At the moment, she felt like she could eat the entire package.

"Tracie, dear, it looks like you bought out the store," Aunt Betty said as she took some of the bags.

"No, I left plenty on their shelves," Tracie said. "I did buy more than I needed to, but you know, Aunt Betty, I feel a junk-food weekend coming on. As a matter of fact, I'm going into the kitchen right now and rip into that bag of chips."

"I have tuna salad sandwiches and freshly squeezed lemonade ready, so wash your hands, and I'll meet you in the kitchen."

Tracie leaned over and kissed Aunt Betty's cheek. Max barked to get their attention. She realized she still had him on the leash. Reaching down, she unhooked his leash and scratched his ears, and then he was off to the kitchen. Tracie couldn't blame him, because she knew Aunt Betty always had water and a treat waiting for him upon their arrival.

Chapter 12

Tracie had walked farther than she'd intended to. She had lost track of time with all the thoughts that consumed her mind. As she and Max were returning to their usual spot on the beach, Max took off at a run. Tracie looked ahead to see what had captured his attention, and she spotted Matt. A smile crossed her face. She didn't call Max back. She let him run ahead to see his—their—new friend.

By the time Tracie caught up to Max, he was settled next to Matt and having his ears scratched. Matt patted the empty space next to him on the beach towel and said, "Hey, Tracie, care to join me?" Tracie responded by taking a seat, mindful to keep a good distance between them.

He had a snack of cheese, crackers, grapes, and water set out for them.

"I walked a lot farther than I'd planned," Tracie said. "It feels good to sit down."

"I've been taking long walks myself these last couple of weeks. This October weather is really nice—not too hot, not too cold. You can walk a good way without realizing how far you've gone, especially when you have a lot on your mind that you're trying to pray through." Matt gestured to his feast. "Would you care for a snack?" he asked.

"I did work up an appetite with that long walk, so, sure," Tracie replied. "This is a thoughtful treat. Thank you."

Matthew had a paper plate loaded up and was handing it to her before she'd even finished her reply. "Thank you, Matt," she said shyly.

"You are welcome, Tracie," he responded with a smile.

Just before Matthew popped a cheese cube into his mouth, he asked Tracie how she was doing and how business was going. After about thirty minutes of relaxed conversation, Matt asked Tracie if she would like to walk over to his place and take a look at the driftwood tables he had completed. Tracie agreed. Matt had already packed the basket back up, so when Tracie stood, he picked up the beach towel, shook off the sand, and folded it up. They took off in the direction opposite of Aunt Betty's house.

Max sat there, looking confused, and Tracie called to him, tapping her hand on her thigh. "Come on, Max. Let's go check out Matt's craftsmanship." Max followed them, and when they got to the steps leading up to the balcony, Max sat down.

Tracie was all the way at the top before she looked back to see Max still sitting at the bottom. Calling him to come had no effect on the dog. He just sat there, looking at her as if to say, "Are you kidding me?" Tracie took off her backpack, unzipped it, and pulled out a bag of dog treats. Max stood and started wagging his tail. "Come on, boy. You want a treat?" she coaxed. The dog took the first step cautiously, looking up at Tracie. She shook the treat bag, and Max took another step, and then another. "You can do it. Come on, boy," Tracie encouraged him. As soon as he reached the top, Tracie scratched his ears and gave him one of his bacon strip treats. She also pulled out his portable bowl and a bottle of water. She popped his bowl into shape and filled it half full. Max had practically inhaled the treat and was now lapping the water. When Tracie looked up, she saw Matt watching her with a smile on his face.

"Was that entertaining?" Tracie asked.

"Yes, as a matter of fact, it was," Matt said. "You are so good with that dog. He listens and obeys you. He seems to trust you so much. Maybe we can learn a lesson from him about listening to God and trusting him in our lives." He chuckled.

"He has been a true companion and friend to me ever since my divorce," Tracie said as she petted Max. "I guess you could say we have a special bond. God knew I needed Max, and Max needed me. He placed us together at just the right time."

Looking to where Matt was standing, Tracie caught a glimpse of the driftwood tables. Moving toward one of them, she said, "Matt, this is really cool. It turned out great." She glanced across the porch to the other table. The design was the same, but the table was different because of the formation of the driftwood—natural and beautiful.

Atop both tables were generic citronella candles. They looked like miniature galvanized washtubs. "Interesting choice of candles for your beach theme," Tracie said with a smile. She gave him a little teasing wink, but of course he couldn't see it, because she still had her sunglasses on. Matt grinned back, informing her that he thought they were a great choice with his folding sports chairs. They both laughed. It was a good feeling. Enjoying this new friendship, Tracie was glad he had come down to the beach and introduced himself to her a few weeks earlier. She prayed that God would guide her steps, because she could get used to the idea of a relationship with Matt.

They chatted for a few more minutes as Matt shared his next project, already in progress. He was making some non-sports chairs for his balcony. They were going to be similar to Adirondack chairs, only they wouldn't lean back quite as far.

Tracie's phone rang, and she thought Aunt Betty was checking on her. She'd been gone longer than anticipated. Digging around in the backpack, she found the phone just as it quit ringing, but not before Nicholas's number had disappeared from the screen, reminding her that she'd told him she would call him back. Ugh. She didn't want to talk to him and spoil her weekend with Matt. The phone's ringing had broken the sweet time she and Matt were having, and that upset her. She needed to get back to Aunt Betty's and call Nicholas to get it over with.

Tracie walked over to the dog's bowl, poured the water out and shook it to release the excess, and tucked it into her backpack.

"Tracie, is everything okay?" Matt asked.

"Yes, fine, why?" she said.

"It seems like that phone call changed the lightness of your mood," he said.

"I really should be going, Matt. I've been gone for a while. Aunt Betty is probably wondering what's keeping me, since I didn't bring my laptop with me."

Matthew nodded, acknowledging her comment, and said, "Yes, she probably is. Speaking of ringing phones, would you mind giving me your phone number, Tracie? A couple of times this past week, I wished I'd asked for it two weeks ago."

"Sure, you can have my number. I'd enjoy hearing from you sometime."

"Let me grab something to write with," Matt said.

As he was turning toward the door, Tracie said, "I can give you one of my business cards tomorrow if you'd like."

"Tomorrow? Are you asking if you can see me tomorrow?"

"Um, yes, tomorrow, right," Tracie responded. "Would you like to come to Aunt Betty's and have lunch with us? She's making one of my favorites: chicken pizzarella."

"Sounds interesting. Are you asking me on a date?" This time Matt smiled and winked at Tracie. She blushed as he laughed. "I'm teasing you, Tracie. I'd love to have lunch with you and Betty tomorrow. What time?"

"One o'clock, if that works for you," Tracie said. "And now I really need to go."

"Okay, I'll see you tomorrow then—about one o'clock."

Tracie called Max and headed down the steps. Going down, Max didn't need to be coaxed.

As Tracie walked the distance between Matt's place and her aunt's house, she prayed, not only asking God to guide her friendship with Matt, but also to guide her conversation with Nicholas. She would call him after dinner.

The Lord will guide you always. He will satisfy your needs in a sun-scorched land and will strengthen your frame. You will be like a well-watered garden, like a spring whose water never fails (Isaiah 58:1).

Chapter 13

The past five weeks had been a blur. The three clients Tracie had been working with had kept her extremely busy. Mrs. Hoppinger had totally changed her mind again. She no longer wanted to change her living room. She'd said that could wait. She now wanted to do her sunroom. The good news was that she had already made a decision on the type décor she wanted. The rectangular room was about twelve by sixteen feet and would be decorated with a beach theme. That would be a breeze, Tracie thought. She'd had a design and a contract ready, signed, sealed, and delivered in a week's time.

Tracie asked Matt if he would be interested in making two more driftwood tables for one of her jobs. She would need one table to be larger—coffee table size—and an end table the same size as the one he'd made for his deck. He seemed flattered that she liked the tables well enough to use in a client's home. Matt also volunteered to deliver it to the job site for her when she was ready for it. Her plans were to have everything in hand and the sunroom complete on the Friday before Thanksgiving, which was the next weekend.

Tracie had just finished the job for Bob, her first male client. Decorating for him had been easy, with the exception of a change in the headboard order. He had recently moved to the area from Dallas, Texas, and was a huge Cowboys fan. He'd wanted his bedroom to reflect the Cowboys' colors—grey and navy—and to be on the contemporary side.

She had found a fabric-covered headboard for his king-size bed. It was done in three pieces, all hooking together. The bottom piece was dark gray, the middle piece was a medium shade of gray, and the top piece was a light gray. The only problem was that it didn't go with the comforter Bob had already purchased and declared perfect. The comforter had navy and gray stripes.

The walls were painted just a tad darker than the lightest color of the fabric in the headboard. The draperies were navy, because Bob had insisted that the blackout style only looked good in dark colors. Bob had walked in, looked around the freshly painted room, and said, "The only thing that might have to change is the headboard order. No big deal, right, Tracie? I'll pay you extra. How's that?" As it turned out, Tracie had already called and changed the headboard order to a solid shade of dark gray on the day Bob had insisted on the striped comforter.

Tracie would not give Bob the details for the accessories she had chosen for the walls. He kept reminding her not to forget that the Dallas Cowboys had the big silver star. He acted like she had never seen a football game in her life—not that Dallas was her favorite. After all, she had to support her home team, the Tampa Bay Buccaneers.

The week that all the furnishings arrived and the accessories were completed, Bob was called out of town on business. Tracie couldn't have been happier. That meant he would not be there when she pulled the room together. She had some surprises for him. He met her at Starbucks on Wednesday morning and gave her the key to his condo. The furniture was delivered that afternoon, and by Friday afternoon, when he met her at his place in Lakewood Ranch, he was beaming at the results. He had only known the color of the wall and what the bed looked like. He knew nothing of the projects Tracie had been working on herself. His beloved Dallas Cowboys' stars were not forgotten. Tracie had made a collage of stars out of wood in different sizes. They were painted in navy, silvery-white, and gray.

She had backed a few of the stars with mirrors. The collage hung on one side of the bed and could be seen when you walked into the room. On the wall opposite the collage of stars hung a framed Dallas Cowboys jersey. It wasn't signed, but he loved it. Beneath the hanging jersey was one of the chrome-and-glass tables he had requested. Only it wasn't square like he'd thought it would be. It was in the shape of a star, twenty-two inches in diameter. On top of the bedside table was a special-ordered lamp made out of a leather football. The base was navy blue, and the shade was silver-gray. Beside it sat Tony Dungy's book *A Quiet Strength.* Because of space, the table on the other side of the bed was a little smaller. It was eighteen inches square, made of glass and chrome, and held only his radio alarm clock.

Bob was so impressed with her work that he not only paid her an extra five hundred dollars for the headboard reorder, which she had told him repeatedly was not necessary, but he also gave her a five-hundred-dollar bonus. That was a thousand dollars over her original bid to him.

And my God will meet all your needs according to the riches of his glory in Christ Jesus (Philippians 4:19 NIV).

May Belle was one of Tracie's other current clients. She was transforming her sitting room to have vintage charm. When Tracie's design was complete, she knew it would look precious and beautiful, just like May Belle. May Belle said, "My husband, bless his soul, only wanted big leather chairs and more of a Gothic flair. I never liked it, but I wouldn't think of going against his wishes."

Tracie would finish May Belle's sitting room the second week in December. The sofa she'd decided on was on back order and wouldn't be delivered until then. Everything else was stored in Tracie's workshop until that time. She could hardly wait to get the vintage room finished. It was going to be charming. The purple vase she had purchased at Home Goods was the same shade as the purple thread outlining the lighter shade of purple in the flowers on the throw pillows she'd found at TJ Maxx. The lighter shades of purple were usually associated with peaceful, warm feelings, while the darker shades created an elegance and royal atmosphere. May Belle was both. Tracie has found a sage-green bowl for the center of the coffee table. It was the same shade of green as the threaded stems and leaves on the throw pillows.

The colors would blend perfectly with the cream color of the sofa and the vintage straight-backed chairs. The chairs were upholstered in soft sage fabric with tufts and buttons on the backs.

Chapter 14

_Tracie talked Mrs. Hoppinger into spending the day at the mall with her friend Madge while her sunroom was being decorated. True to her word, she was ready to leave when Tracie arrived at her house on Friday morning at nine. The only thing that had changed was the destination: Mrs. Hoppinger was having a "spa day" instead of a mall day. Tracie was not surprised by the change of plans, considering the older lady's indecisiveness.

The delivery of the furniture was right on schedule at ten o'clock. Tracie had the delivery driver remove all the brown paper and plastic from the furnishings so she could inspect each piece before she signed off on the receipt. She was thankful it was all in perfect condition.

The sunroom was accessible from the living areas, separated by French doors. Entry was also available from the master bedroom. Her client had told her she seldom used the bedroom entrance to the room and asked if something could be done to cover the sliding glass door there. Tracie had made a window covering to hang on the wall that housed the sliding door. The back was made from a brocade fabric the same shade as the sand color of the walls. In front of that fabric she had sewn a sheer fabric of multiple shades of blues and greens. Once they were hung, Tracie was pleased; they looked just as she had envisioned they would. From a distance, it looked like the sea. With the ceiling fan on, the breeze gently moved the sheer fabric, giving the effect of gentle waves. Tracie had found a CD with the sounds of the ocean and had popped it into the stereo, which gave the full effect of the ocean.

With the window treatment done to her satisfaction, she turned her attention to the sofa and ottoman. They were rattan and painted a shade or two darker than the walls. The cushions were aquamarine in color. Decorative pillows sat in both corners of the sofa. The pillows were the color of sand with a design of multicolored shells, starfish, and seahorses. On the far side of the room sat the distressed green wrought-iron, sixty-inch, round table and matching chairs. The fabric on the cushions matched the pillows on the sofa. The room was really coming together.

Tracie heard the doorbell ring and looked at her watch. It was high noon, which meant it would be Matt with the driftwood tables. She walked to the door. She could hardly wait to see his handiwork. His table would be the piece that pulled the room together. She opened the door to see Matt standing there with his hands in his pockets and a smile on his face. Suddenly, butterflies filled her stomach. She felt nervous and couldn't seem to find her voice.

Matt said, "Hey, Tracie."

She just stared at him. He looked great. His blue eyes matched the golf shirt, and that smile …

"Hel-looooo, Tracie?" Matt called out.

Feeling slightly embarrassed, Tracie responded, "Hi, um, hey, Matt. I'm sorry, I must have been daydreaming for a minute. Come in, please." She stepped aside to let him in.

"Daydreaming about me?" he asked with that killer smile as he stepped across the threshold and winked at her.

Tracie didn't answer his question. She stepped in front of him and led him to the sunroom.

"Come and tell me what you think," she said to him over her shoulder.

"I think you look beautiful, even in jeans and a T-shirt," he said.

"Even with that little smudge of dirt right here on your nose." He reached up and wiped at the mark with his finger.

She felt the color rise in her cheeks. She asked, "Did you have any trouble finding the place? Did you wrap the glass top with the bubble wrap and packing blankets I left you last weekend?"

"No to the first question, yes to the second," Matt said. "You sure know how to change the subject quickly." He turned around, taking in all that she had done with the room. "Looking good. I'm talking about the room now." He gave her another wink.

"It's all coming together," Tracie responded. "I have some accessories in my car. The seahorse should be arriving any minute now. Ed from the gallery told me he would hang it for me."

"I'll go get the tables from the truck, and then I'll help you get the things from your car," Matt said as he headed toward the front door.

"I only have a couple of boxes," Tracie said. "I can get them while you're getting the tables."

Tracie's phone rang just as she opened her car door to pull out the boxes. She saw Ella's face on the screen and answered. "Hey, little girl. Can you hold on just a minute?" She turned to Matt, held up the phone, and said, "It's Ella. I'll only be a few minutes." She turned her back to Matt and continued her phone conversation. Ella wanted her to know that her dad would be at the Thanksgiving Day dinner she was hosting. Bless her heart, she always tried to make sure Tracie knew ahead of time if she was going to be seeing Nicholas.

After several minutes, Matt walked over to Tracie's car, retrieved the two small boxes from her back seat, and took them inside. Tracie saw the art gallery truck coming down the road and told Ella she had to go.

Ed hopped out of the truck and said, "Hey, Tracie, just show me where you want these things, and I'll be done in no time at all."

Once Ed had hung the artwork and was gone, Tracie looked at the driftwood tables and then at Matt. They were perfect. She moved to the far left of the room to see the thirty-two-inch seahorse Ed had mounted on the wall. She turned to Matt, and before giving it any thought, she threw her arms around Matt's neck and gave him a huge hug. "Thank you, Matt. They're perfect!"

She stepped back and looked up at him. A tear escaped from her eye and ran down her cheek. He reached down and cupped her face with his hands and wiped the tear away. His intense blue eyes never left hers.

"It's beautiful, isn't it?" she said.

He placed a hand on her shoulder and said, "It certainly is."

She liked his touch but felt a bit awkward at the same time. With a flick of her wrist, she looked at her watch. It was two o'clock. She stepped back and said, "Oh, my, look at the time. Mrs. Hoppinger will be back in an hour. I have to get busy placing the accessories. I'll go and retrieve that last box from my trunk." With that she was out the door.

Matthew followed her, saying, "I have a few errands to run— Walmart, Lowe's, the bank. Why don't I take care of that while you finish up here? Then maybe we could meet up at Starbucks for coffee. I noticed one just down the road west of the interstate."

"That sounds good," Tracie said. "After I get out of here, I'll need a cup of coffee. Hopefully, I can be done and out of here by four. Does that give you enough time to get the things on your list done?"

"Sure. I'll see you about four thirty then," Matt said.

"Okay. And Matt, again, thank you so much."

He turned and headed toward his truck, saying, "You are very welcome."

Tracie headed back inside, lamp in tow. It was a glass cylinder on a sand-colored base. She had filled the inside with shells she'd collected from the beach. The lamp looked nice atop the small driftwood table. She placed a large conch shell candle in the middle of the larger coffee table in front of the sofa. On one end she put the starfish and seashell coaster set she'd found at a little specialty shop the last time she and Aunt Betty had gone to downtown Venice for lunch. On the other end she placed a book about Florida beaches.

The only thing left to do was to hang the resin dolphins and starfish on the wall by the big round table.

Just as she was straightening the last dolphin, Mrs. Hoppinger walked in. She just stared, her eyes shifting from one side of the room to the other. Finally she said, "Tracie, you have outdone yourself. This room is absolutely perfect. I wouldn't change a thing. The tables are amazing. I've never seen any like them. Thank you so much. Now, let me get my checkbook and settle up with you."

Chapter 15

_Tracie saw Matt sitting at a table in the back corner of Starbuck's when she walked in. She ordered a skinny vanilla latte with half the sweet, and then she joined him. He rose as she approached the table, pulled out the chair for her, and asked, "How did it go?"

"Great! Mrs. Hoppinger was almost speechless when she walked in." Tracie sat down.

"Tracie, you've worked so hard these past few weeks. Why don't you go home and relax tonight?"

"Maybe I'll do that," she answered. "I plan to stay at Aunt Betty's until Wednesday anyway. Then I'll come back and see if Ella needs help with the Thanksgiving meal preparations."

"I'm very glad to hear that," Matt said.

"Are you now? Why is that?" Tracie asked.

"Well, since you asked …" Matt paused for a moment and looked down at Tracie's hand on the table. He reached over and covered it with his, looked back up at her, and said, "I enjoy spending time with you. I like you, Tracie—a lot. I'd like the opportunity to get to know you better."

"Matthew, I, um, I don't know what to say." Tracie felt the color rise in her cheeks.

"At least you consider me a friend," he said.

"Of course I do. Why would you say that?" she asked.

"You just called me Matthew instead of Matt." He gave her hand a little squeeze.

Tracie was just about to respond, when she saw Nicholas walking toward them. She slid her hand out from under Matthew's and put it in her lap. As he approached the table, he said, "Hello, Tracie."

She felt like she was going to be sick. She liked Matthew. She had been praying about their friendship going to the next level. She had never anticipated a meeting between Nicholas and Matthew right now. What lousy timing this was! Matthew liked her. Why did Nicholas have to show up now and complicate things?

"Tracie?" Nicholas repeated, bringing her back from her thoughts.

"Nicholas, I'm surprised to see you at this end of town," Tracie said.

"Aren't you going to introduce me to your friend?" he pressed.

Tracie could not believe he had the audacity to approach her as if he was her close friend. She had been doing her best to avoid him and to ignore his phone calls.

Using hand gestures, she said, "Nicholas, my friend Matthew. Matthew, Nicholas."

Matthew, being the gentleman he was, rose to his feet and reached out to shake Nicholas's hand.

"So, do you mind if I pull up a chair and—"

Tracie interrupted by holding her hand up. "Nicholas, this is not a good time, and yes, I do mind if you pull up a chair. Matthew and I are in the middle of a personal conversation."

"Oh, sorry. Well, I'll see you Thursday for dinner then, okay?" Nicholas asked, his gaze going toward Matthew and then back to Tracie.

"I will be at Ella's on Thanksgiving Day, if that's what you're referring to, Nicholas," she said.

After he walked away, Tracie looked at Matthew. She took a deep breath and exhaled slowly.

"Your ex, I take it," Matthew said.

Tracie nodded. "I thought this would be a safe place to have coffee and a chat. Next time, we should just go to my place, and I'll make coffee."

"I'm glad to hear there will be a next time," Matthew teased, winking at her.

"I'd suggest you come over now, and we can order pizza or get Chinese takeout," she said, "but I've pretty much monopolized your day already."

"I guess that's not really an invitation then, is it?" Matthew asked.

"It could be, if ..." Tracie paused.

"If what? If you thought I would accept?"

"Yes, I suppose," Tracie responded with a blush.

"I don't want to seem forward or make you feel like you should ask me to come over, Tracie, but if you did, I would say yes. I know you're tired and need to rest after such a busy week, so don't feel obligated to ask. I'll look forward to spending more time with you over the next several weeks."

Tracie looked up and smiled. She said, "I look forward the coming month as well. But I know the ferry runs up until ten p.m. tonight, and it's only five o'clock, so if you would like to join me at the house for a while, I'd love to have the company."

Matthew said yes, along with a little hand pump, and winked at her.

The weekend at Aunt Betty's went by much too quickly. They prepared the traditional turkey dinner with all the trimmings on Sunday. Aunt Betty was going with Tracie to Ella's on Wednesday and Thursday where they would have the feast again. They had talked about having something different on Sunday, but since Matthew had no family, they wanted him to have a traditional Thanksgiving meal. Tracie would have liked to invite him to Ella's, but she didn't think the timing was right. She knew Nicholas would be putting the pressure on. Matthew's presence would have been a nice distraction, but she was not up to that confrontation just yet.

Tracie and Matthew walked the beach on Monday. The weather was a little cool, so jeans and lightweight jackets were the attire. Max, of course, was with them and running ahead as if to clear the path.

Matthew invited Tracie and Aunt Betty over for spaghetti the following evening. Aunt Betty declared she had a headache and told Tracie to go and enjoy her evening. She wanted to rest up for the festivities at Ella's.

Tracie wasn't really buying the headache story, but she was looking forward to spending the evening with Matthew. She had a gift for him, for his deck. While shopping for Mrs. Hoppinger's beach-themed sunroom, she had found the perfect candles for his driftwood tables. Now he could get rid of his little washtub candles. Smiling to herself, she picked up the box that held the gift, kissed her aunt's cheek, started for the golf cart, and headed the short distance to Matthew's.

The aroma drifting out of his house as she climbed the steps to the deck made her mouth water. She remembered that she had not had lunch. She had written some in her book that afternoon and had been so engrossed, she'd forgotten to stop and eat.

When she reached the deck, Matthew stepped out the back door to greet her. Seeing the box she carried, he asked, "What have we here?"

Tracie said, "It's a token of appreciation for your help at Mrs. Hoppinger's the other day."

"You shouldn't have," he said as he opened the box. When he saw the conch shell citronella candles, he said, "Tracie, these are perfect." He set one on each of the driftwood tables and removed the little washtub candles. That was when Tracie noticed the four Adirondack chairs. They were awesome! Each was a different color: teal, orange, red, and bright yellow.

"Matthew, the chairs are great! I love the colors. This deck is really taking on the look of a beach house deck."

Chapter 16

Tracie prayed without ceasing on the way to Ella's house on Thanksgiving morning. She expected Nicholas to hound her for information about Matthew. The last time she'd seen him was when she'd been at Starbuck's with Matt. Nicholas had called her four times. She'd let all the calls go to voice mail and had not returned any of them.

She prayed that today would be uneventful, just a nice, relaxing meal with her family. She prayed that Nicholas would realize that this was not the time or place for questioning her.

After parking in Ella's driveway, she stayed in the car for a few minutes to text Matthew. Then she gathered up her keys, purse, and the pumpkin pies. The pies where the only request Ella had asked of her for the day. As she exited her vehicle, she was startled when she almost literally ran into Nicholas.

"Nicholas, I didn't see you there," she said.

"I didn't think you did, since you almost ran me over," he said. "Here, let me help you." He took the load of pies from her arms.

Tracie had just raised her hand to knock, when Jason opened the door. He stepped back to let them in, saying, "Tracie, Nicholas, Happy Thanksgiving. Did you come together?" Then he yelled over his shoulder, "Ella, your parents are here."

"No, no, of course not, Jason," Tracie responded, but no one heard her over the commotion that followed. Bailey came running from one end of the house, shouting, "Gramma, Grampa, you're both here, together."

Ella walked out from the kitchen, drying her hands on her turkey apron, the only apron she ever wore. "Mom, Dad, so good to see you both," she said as she leaned in to give each of them a kiss on the cheek. Tracie took the pies from Nicholas and followed Ella back into the kitchen. "It's not what it looks like, Ella," Tracie said.

"What's not?" Aunt Betty asked, looking up from the table where she sat snapping the green beans for dinner.

"Aunt Betty, hi. Are you enjoying your stay with Ella and Bailey?" she asked her aunt.

"Oh, yes, it's been delightful," her aunt replied. "I need to come visit more often. Bailey has been teaching me how to use my new cell phone. I never knew there was so much I could do on it. And that game, Candy Crush—well, it's so much fun trying to figure out which candy to move next. Keeps the mind young."

Tracie hoped her aunt was distracted enough to forget the question she had just asked.

Jason and Nicholas entered the kitchen. Ella had popovers and coffee already set on the table, along with butter, honey, apple butter, and strawberry preserves.

As they ate, conversations ranged from Tracie's latest decorating jobs to Bailey's basketball games, Jason's new truck, and Ella's wonderfully scented candles filling the house with holiday aroma.

After brunch was cleared from the table and the dishes were put away, Tracie said, "If you'll excuse me, I'm going to step out on the patio and make a call."

"Mom, you're not taking care of business today, are you?" Ella asked.

"No, honey, I'm only checking on a friend. I won't be long."

Tracie had just said goodbye to Matthew when Nicholas joined her on the patio. She had watched him coming outside, and before he could say a word, she looked him straight in the eye and said, "Nicholas, why did you lead everyone to believe we came here together?"

"I didn't say a word, Tracie," he replied.

"I know. When Jason assumed we had come together, you should have told him differently."

"No harm done. I'm sure they didn't give it a second thought," he said, making light of the situation.

"Are you kidding me? Didn't you see the way Bailey and Ella came running from opposite ends of the house when they heard Jason's announcement? Don't give them false hope, Nicholas." She started past him to go inside.

"It's not a false hope, unless you're seeing the coffee shop guy," he said with a sly grin.

"That, Nicholas, is none of your business," she stated and went back inside.

The Thanksgiving feast was delicious. Nicholas had not said another word to Tracie about personals matters. The guys headed to the family room to watch the football game, and the ladies cleaned the kitchen, putting away the leftovers in Ziploc bags.

The ladies had been enjoying lighthearted conversation when the guys wandered back into the living room. Ella looked up and asked, "Is the game over?"

"Yes," Jason replied. "Our team was on the losing end today."

"Well, would you look at the time?" Tracie said. "Thank you, Ella and Jason, for a lovely Thanksgiving Day." She gave Bailey a hug and told Aunt Betty she would be by on Saturday morning to take her back home.

Nicholas also rose to say his goodbyes. Much to Tracie's surprise, he looked at Ella and said, "Although your mom and I did not come together, I need to be going as well.

Christmas came and went rapidly. Tracie spent most of her time at the beach house, leaving only to finish May Belle's sitting room. When she wasn't working on her book, she was walking the beach with Matthew. They had some long conversations about their pasts and their goals for the future.

Matthew had been the perfect gentleman, praying for the right timing and God's will. Tracie had not wanted to move into a relationship quickly.

Nicholas had started sending Tracie flowers just before Christmas. After sending the last ones, peach-colored roses, her favorite—or they used to be—he called her again the next day. Tracie answered and said, "Nicholas, what are you doing? Why all the flowers? I thought they would stop if I ignored your calls."

"Now, Tracie, is that any way to answer your phone?" Nicholas responded with teasing in his voice. "Most people say hello before they speak a full sentence or two."

Before she could say anything else, he began again. "Tracie, all I do is think about you, day and night. I can't sleep. I can't eat. I'm hoping you will at least talk to me over dinner one evening and let me try to explain some things to you. Are you going to Betty's tomorrow?"

She had not been expecting this. She had thought he was only trying to woo her because he'd seen her with Matthew before Thanksgiving. She'd thought Nicholas was only trying to find out if she was seeing Matthew—or if he was a client. But Nicholas hadn't asked. Besides, she wanted him to suffer a little, to feel a small measure of the heart-wrenching pain he had caused her. Then she reeled her thoughts back in. Hadn't she forgiven him? Yes, she had. It was a daily battle sometimes, but yes, she had forgiven him.

"No, Nicholas, I have a meeting with a potential client tomorrow, so I won't be going to Aunt Betty's."

"Would you please consider having dinner with me tomorrow evening, then? Please?"

"I'm not sure that's a good idea, Nicholas," she responded.

"Tracie, my divorce is final, if that's what concerns you. Unless you're seeing someone else."

Tracie didn't respond. She just let out a long sigh, and Nicholas pleaded, "No pressure, Tracie. Just dinner and conversation, please."

After a few moments of his persistence, Tracie gave in. She agreed to dinner. She did not, however, agree to let him pick her up. It was settled: she would meet him at Marina Jack's at 6:00 p.m. They would be taking the Marina Jack II dinner boat.

"What was I thinking?" Tracie scolded herself aloud. Things had been slowly progressing with Matthew. She really liked him. So, why was she agreeing to have dinner with Nicolas? This was ludicrous.

On Saturday morning Tracie met with the Malones, a nice family who had just relocated from Ohio. They told Tracie the move had been difficult for their three children. The house they'd purchased had been newly renovated, and they'd promised their children they could decorate their rooms as the chose—within reason, Mrs. Malone said. They had given each child a budget of $3,500.

This, of course, would include the designer's fee. Ten thousand dollars to decorate three rooms was very doable. Tracie would have to shop smart, and she prayed that the children would warm up to her quickly, as that would make it easier to discover their likes and dislikes. She would meet with the kids one-on-one next week to get their thoughts, ideas, and color schemes.

Later that afternoon, while Tracie was getting ready to go and meet Nicholas, she was half talking to herself and half praying. "Why in the world did I ever agree to this? My goodness, I think I've lost my mind."

Back and forth to the closet she went, pulling out one blouse and then another, talking to herself all the while. "Lord, why would I do something like this. I don't want him to be back in my life. Do I?

Oh, my goodness, I do. No, no, Lord, I don't. It would never work out. It wouldn't be the same. I can't go back. I need to call Alice. Oh, no, I don't. I didn't even tell her about this. She would read me the riot act or come over and kidnap me so I couldn't go at all. She's going to be livid when she finds out about this one. Whoa! Tracie was getting herself all worked up, and the best thing she knew to do was to stop everything and pray. And that was exactly what she did.

She went to the corner chair in her bedroom, sat down, opened her Bible to the book of Psalms, and began reading. The psalms always seemed to calm her. After reading a couple of chapters, she set the Bible aside, slid to the floor, got on her knees, and began praying.

"Dear heavenly Father, I know I do things without thinking sometimes and without asking for your guidance. Your word tells me to ask. You are the good shepherd who will take care of me. I don't want to do anything in my life without first consulting with you, asking and waiting for your response. When I don't, there seem to be challenges at every turn. I have committed to this dinner tonight, and I ask you to calm me and give me peace. Help me get through this night. Amen."

Tracie decided on the forest-green sweater and winter-white dress slacks. She finished applying makeup and ran the hot curling iron through her hair to give it a lift. After spraying a squirt of "Lovely," her favorite perfume, on her neck and wrist, she finished off with her rose lip gloss and was out the door.

Nicholas was waiting for her when she walked up to the dock at the Marina Jack II. Thank goodness, it was a mild January, and lows were going to be in the mid sixties. It was typical for Florida at this time of year.

They were seated on the main level. The waiter had taken their order, poured their wine, and left the table. Nicholas looked at her with such longing and a gentle smile. The sun had gone down, and the candle flickering on the table put an angelic glow on his handsome face. Tracie had to look away. A feeling she had not expected overtook her. All of a sudden, she felt like she was living in the past, twenty years earlier. She had a desire to reach up and caress his face, to kiss him, to be held by him.

"Tracie," Nicholas whispered, "are you okay?"

"Yeah, um, I'm fine," she replied.

"For a minute there, you looked a thousand miles away," he said.

"No, I was just—will you excuse me a moment, Nicholas? I need to find the ladies' room." Tracie rose from her chair, not waiting for a response, and made a beeline to the restroom. She prayed the whole time that God would give her the strength and courage to return to the table and get this evening behind her. Not wanting to alarm him by being gone too long, she dabbed her teary eyes and pinched her cheeks to gain some color that had been lost between the table and the restroom. Then she reapplied her lip gloss and headed back to the table.

As soon as she sat down, Tracie asked Nicholas what was on his mind. "Why all the flowers and phone calls?"

Nicholas paused. Looking at her, he said, "You look beautiful tonight. The sweater really brings out the green in your eyes. I've always thought your eyes were awesome "cat eyes." You remember me telling you that, don't you? The forest green really enhances them."

"Thank you, Nicholas, for the compliment, but I'm sure you didn't ask me out tonight to talk about my sweater or my eye color." Tracie tried not to sound sarcastic. She had a way of doing that when she put up her guard.

Nicholas began to explain the way he had felt before leaving her. He apologized for the pain, heartache, and shattered dreams he had caused not only her but Ella. He stopped briefly as the waiter brought their food and refilled their water and wine glasses, and then he started again. He told her he'd had regrets from day one about leaving her, but he hadn't known how to right his wrong. He continued talking as tears began to slide down his cheeks.

Tracie wanted to stop him, wanted him to continue, wanted to comfort him. But she also wanted him to feel a small fraction of the turmoil he'd caused in her heart and mind. Still, she couldn't seem to stop herself as she reached over with the back of her hand and wiped the tears from his cheek.

He took her hand and stood up. He asked her to go outside on the upper deck with him. The moon was full, the night clear. He put his arm around her as she shivered a bit. He turned her to face him, and she knew she should turn her face away. But she couldn't. His gentle kiss made her weak in the knees. She pulled away from this kiss but did not leave his embrace. She laid her head on his shoulder. For several minutes, neither of them spoke. Tracie finally pulled away and said, "Our dinner is getting cold." She started back inside to the lower deck.

Their food was as cold as the turn the conversation was taking.

"I didn't think you had started dating again," Nicholas said, "but that guy I saw you with at Starbucks looked like more than a causal acquaintance."

"He is a friend, but really, Nicholas, don't concern yourself with my personal life. I would rather talk about something else."

"I hit a nerve, didn't I?" he asked.

"Nicholas, please, don't. Who I spend my time with, or my friends, are not up for discussion." Her response was firm.

"I'm sorry, Tracie. I was out of line. I have no right asking you questions about your life." He changed the subject. "Tell me about your decorating business. You seem to enjoy it."

The rest of their conversation revolved around Ella, Jason, and Bailey.

Chapter 17

It had been two weeks since Tracie had been to the beach house. Now she was finally on her way. She was ready to relax. She had no plans to write or work on the Malone children's room designs this weekend. R and R—that was what she needed. And time to pray.

Praying was so what she needed to do. She had not seen Nicholas since the Marina Jack II dinner boat, but they had talked almost every day. Now she was going to see Matthew.

She was so confused. She had a great relationship with Matthew. She knew he was ready to take their relationship to the next level. She'd thought that was what she wanted as well—until that evening two weeks ago with Nicholas. She was so mixed up, not only in her head but in her heart was well. Tracie had read 1 Corinthians 14:33 over and over—in two different versions of the Bible. The ESV said, "For God is not a God of confusion but of peace." The KJV said, "For God is not the author of confusion, but of peace."

Tracie knew that the enemy of her soul wanted her to be confused. She also knew that God wanted her to have peace. When she thought about life with Matthew or Nicholas, fear started to set in. She was afraid of being hurt again. She also knew that 2 Timothy 1:7 (NKJV) said, "For God has not given us a spirit of fear, but of power and of love and of a sound mind."

Knowing these truths deep in her heart and spirit, she was determined not to move forward in her relationship with either

Matthew or Nicholas until she was sure she had heard from God and knew what his will for her life was.

Tracie felt like she was living a life of deceit. Matthew did not know about her date or recent conversations with Nicholas, and Nicholas did not know about her association with Matthew. It was time she was honest with Matthew. His response might help her sort things out. She would share her thoughts with him tonight at dinner.

It was Valentine's Day, and Matthew had made reservations at a restaurant in town. He loved having dinner with Tracie's aunt, but he wanted to have some time alone with Tracie, since he hadn't seen her for two weeks. He had purchased a beautiful fourteen-carat gold necklace with double interlocking hearts. He wanted to give that to her tonight—and to share his growing feelings for her. This was not something he'd just jumped into. He had been fasting and praying ever since the first day he'd met her. He had felt God's peace and knew he wanted to take their friendship to the next level. Matthew had had coffee with Tracie's aunt the day before. He'd told her he planned to ask Tracie to be his girl. Aunt Betty had been delighted and had given him her blessing.

At the restaurant that evening, Tracie was unusually quiet. Halfway through their meal, Matthew asked, "So, sweet girl, tell me what's been troubling you?" Tracie had determined in her heart not to cry, but as she looked up at Matthew, tears began to fall. Matthew reached across the table, took her face in his hands, and wiped away the tears with his thumbs. "Ah, Tracie, what is it?" he asked gently.

"Matthew, I haven't been totally honest with you," she replied.

"What do you mean?" he asked. "Is it Nicholas?"

She nodded.

"What exactly does that mean? Are you seeing him again?"

Tracie's response was accompanied by more tears. "No, I mean yes, I saw him once. Two weeks ago."

"Does this mean you're seeing him? That you want to get back together with him?" Matthew asked. Suddenly he no longer had an appetite. He motioned to the waiter for their check. "Do you mind if we go back to my place and talk?" he asked.

"I would like that," she said.

They drove the short distance from the restaurant to the ferry. Once they were back at Matthew's house, Tracie shared with him what had transpired and told him she was very confused. She told him she knew confusion was not of God and she had been praying about the situation. She told him she really enjoyed spending time with him too. She let him know that fear was gripping her heart because she didn't want to be hurt again. By this time, Tracie was sobbing.

Matthew drew her into an embrace. He held her and let her have the time she needed to release the pent-up emotions. When she raised her head, he told her, "In 2 Timothy 1:7 it says that God has not given us a spirit of fear, but of love, power, and a sound mind."

Then he took her hand and began to pray that God would give her clarity of mind and peace. He also prayed that she would know the will of God for her life. They spent a couple of hours talking and sharing scripture. Matthew encouraged her to follow God—and then her heart.

Chapter 18

Tracie knew she needed some unbiased, godly advice, so on Monday she called Peggie, her counselor. Peggie had had a four o'clock cancellation and could see her that afternoon.

During their session, Tracie told Peggie about the night on the Marina Jack II with Nicholas, and about the night she'd shared it all with Matthew. Peggie told her that Nicholas was not the same man she had married all those years ago. Peggie asked her to think about what he had shared that night on the dinner boat. It had been an apology, not a proposal. She asked Tracie if she could trust that he would not do the same thing to her again one day, if they got back together. More importantly, had he confessed his sin and asked God to forgive him, or only Tracie?

Peggie went on to point out Matthew's response: scripture (the word of God) and prayer. Peggie told Tracie she needed to get into the word herself, to fast and pray and not to act until she heard from God. "God is peace, Tracie, not confusion," Peggie said. "The enemy wants to keep you in a state of confusion, because it will keep you away from God." The two women prayed together and scheduled another meeting for mid-March.

When Nicholas called later that evening, Tracie asked him to give her some space. She told him she wanted to spend the next two weeks fasting, praying, and seeking God's will for her life.

Nicholas's response surprised her. He asked, "Tracie, you don't really believe that God has a specific plan for your life, do you?"

"Of course I do, Nicholas. Don't you?" she responded.

"I use to, Tracie, but now I don't know. My life is in such disarray."

"Nicholas, that's because of the choices you've made. You weren't walking in God's perfect plan for your life."

She couldn't imagine that Nicholas didn't believe this. He'd used to be a believer. They had never missed a Sunday service and had attended some Wednesday nights. Nicholas had even gone on some mission trips. She was shocked at his response.

"Nicholas, you once believed the same way I believe," she said. "We raised our daughter to trust and serve the Lord. You know God is merciful and full of grace. We have seen him work miracles in the lives of our family and friends. Yes, I believe every written word in the Bible, Nicholas." Then she told him she was taking the next two weeks to fast, pray, and seek God's will for her life. She would not be going to the beach house during that time, either.

Matthew's response had been so different from Nicholas's. He had told Tracie he would miss her desperately, but he understood. He said he would be fasting and praying as well.

For the next couple of weeks, Tracie poured herself into her work. When she wasn't working, she was in the word and praying. Worship music filled her house. Her mind was consumed with the goodness of God.

Tracie would catch herself thinking about Nicholas and the things he'd said. He had vowed that he loved her and wanted a fresh start. She only allowed herself to stay in those thoughts briefly, and then she would begin praying fervently.

She thought of Matthew too, often comparing him with Nicholas in her mind. She would not let her mind dwell there, either. Then she would fall on her knees, open her worn Bible, seek God, and pray again and again.

During her prayer time on the morning she was scheduled to

meet with Peggie, she had a peace wash over her. She was reminded of all the ways that Matthew had responded to conversations and situations, always directing her to seek God, always praying for guidance. He had prayed with her and for her, asking the Lord to direct her steps. She was reminded of the negative, ungodly behavior of Nicholas. She knew which way God was leading, and she couldn't wait to talk with Peggie.

When she shared with Peggie the way Nicholas had acted when she'd asked for space, Peggie asked, "How did that make you feel?" Tracie didn't respond. Peggie looked at her with a smile and said, "Do I have to get the 'feelings wheel' out again?"

Tracie chuckled. Peggie had used that color wheel many times with her in the past. That was when Nicholas had first left and she could barely feel anything, much less put the feeling into a category.

Tracie looked up at Peggie. "*Disbelief* was not what I expected. I should have known immediately that Nicholas was not the man I'd once loved. He has definitely changed." Tracie could never share her life with him again. He did not believe in the things she did. The Bible said not to be unequally yoked, and they would surely be that if she pursued a relationship with him.

Matthew, on the other hand, was an encourager. He was a believer. He prayed. He read his Bible daily and sought God.

Peggie talked for a little while longer, saying, "I think it is very clear which direction the Lord is leading you. Matthew is the strong man of God that you need in your life. I still would not rush to the altar, though. Take a year. Let him court you. Become better acquainted with each other, and allow God to lead your steps. They prayed together, and Tracie left feeling that a load had been lifted from her shoulders.

Matthew was certainly the type of man that Tracie had been asking God to send her. She just hoped she hadn't waited too long to let him know how she felt. She would call him tonight and ask him if he was free for dinner on Friday night. She was taking Friday morning to run some errands, and then she would be heading to the beach house. Aunt Betty had gone to visit Tracie's dad in North Carolina, so she would have the beach to herself. She had talked to Aunt Betty a couple of times this past week in her distress over the decision she had to make.

After one more phone call, Tracie was headed to bed for a long-needed rest. Her heart was at peace. She called her dad and talked to him briefly, and then he handed the phone to Aunt Betty. Tracie told her aunt about the visit with Peggie and her advice.

Chapter 19

Tracie had met with the Malone children the previous week. Not being able to go forward in her current state of mind, she had taken a lot of notes, getting a feel for each child's likes and personalities.

First she'd met with Daniel. He was the oldest at sixteen. Moving during the middle of his junior year had really been rough on him. He was a stylish young man. His hair was deep brown with lots of natural auburn highlights. His eyes were green with flecks of gold. He was dressed in Aeropostale jeans and a gray-green T-shirt with flip-flops on his feet.

Tracie asked him about his hobbies, likes, dislikes, favorite color, foods, etc., just trying to get him to open up and feel comfortable sharing with her. She took notes while he talked. She found out that he liked to go by his given name of Daniel, but his parents continued to call him by his childhood nickname of Danny. His classmates called him Dan. Depending on their mood, his sisters call him Dan, Danny, or Daniel, but mostly Danny.

Daniel's favorite color was light blue, although he was fond of red too. He loved football and had been accepted on the varsity football team as a running back. He tried to stay fit and ate a healthy, balanced diet. He loved burgers and fries, pizza, and chocolate Moose Tracks ice cream, but he limited them in his daily diet.

Daniel wanted to go back to Ohio and attend college at Ohio State University. His parents were in agreement with that as long as he kept his grades up and earned at least a partial scholarship. Otherwise, he would have to attend a Florida university to keep tuition cost down.

He wanted his room to reflect his passion for Ohio State. Tracie asked if there was anything he liked about Sarasota. His response was "flip-flops and the beach." Tracie shared her fondness of the beach with him as well.

Next, Tracie met with Nicole. Her parents called her Nikki, which she was fine with. Nikki was fourteen and in the eighth grade. Her hair was just below her shoulders, full and very blonde. She wore it down most of the time, expect when she was ice skating. Then she pulled it back into a pony tail or tight bun. She loved to ice skate and had taken lessons since she was four. She was grateful for JP Igloo where she could continue taking lessons, although she missed the openness and freedom of the frozen lakes and ponds she'd skated on during the Ohio winters.

Nikki was more of a loner than Daniel. When she wasn't skating, she usually had her nose in a book. She said the move was "not too bad." Her favorite color was pink—more light pinks than dark. She liked shimmer and sparkle and was fond of antiques. She loved cheeseburgers but had exchanged them for turkey burgers in order to keep her trim shape for the ice. She said any extra pounds made a big difference when skating.

Last, but not least, Tracie met seven-year-old Josie, a joyful, bouncy redhead. Josie wasn't short for Josephine or any other name; it was just Josie. She had her own fashion sense. Dressed in a flared pink-and-white polka-dot top and neon-green-and-orange-plaid leggings, she skipped into the office where Tracie was waiting for her.

Josie's big, blue eyes shone with excitement as she told Tracie about her new friend Lucy. As soon as her room was finished, Lucy was coming for a sleepover.

Josie new exactly what she wanted in her room. Her favorite colors were orange and green in almost any shades, and she wanted them incorporated in her room. She wanted a bunk bed—a full-size bed on top with a playhouse underneath—and she wanted it to look like a barn, "like Granddad's barn back home," she said. Tracie made a note to ask her parents for pictures.

Josie wanted a desk where she would have a designated study space, because her mom said she was easily distracted. She loved pizza and chocolate cake and would have eaten them every day, but her mom wouldn't let her.

"And if ya know how to paint good," Josie added, out of the blue, "I want a wall with animals like horses and a dog on it, and maybe a chicken or two."

Tracie laughed out loud. "You're a girl who knows what she wants. I like that."

"Yep," Josie said. " Can ya do it? Can you?"

"I think we might be able to work something out," Tracie replied. Josie was so energetic it wore Tracie out.

After meeting with the three children, Tracie met briefly with Mrs. Malone—or Sheri, as she preferred to be called. Sheri led Tracie to the children's bedrooms where she took all the measurements she needed to get started on the design plan for each room. She told Sheri the meetings with the children had been very helpful. She had lots of ideas and would get a preliminary design together for the three rooms. She asked Sheri if she had any pictures of the barn Josie had referred to. Sheri excused herself, and in a couple of minutes she was back with some pictures from their home in Ohio as well as her parents' farm.

Tracie scheduled another meeting during the latter part of the next week to go over the design plans. First she needed to take refuge at the beach to recharge herself mentally and spiritually.

Chapter 20

*M*idmorning on Friday, Tracie was almost to Aunt Betty's door when she thought she smelled her aunt's awesome blueberry muffins. She shook her head as if to clear it, knowing that her aunt was still in Virginia. She couldn't possibly be smelling those wonderful muffins. "It must just be that I'm so hungry," Tracie said aloud.

Max, as usual, had been running ahead of her. She looked up and saw that the front door was open—and Max had gone in. Alarmed, she starting yelling for Max. Fear set in for just a brief moment, and then she saw Aunt Betty in the doorway. By this point, Tracie was only four feet from the door. She gasped and then let out her breath. "Aunt Betty, you scared me half to death!"

"Tracie, I'm sorry," Betty said. "I was hoping to surprise you, not scare you. I thought you would smell the muffins and realize I came home early."

"Well, I thought I smelled your muffins, but I didn't think you were home, so I thought it was my mind playing tricks on me because I'm starving." She set her stuff down just inside the door and gave her aunt a big hug. "I'm very glad to see you, Aunt Betty, but next time give me a heads up!"

"Well, honey, after talking to you the other night, it sounded like you had things settled in your mind. But I know that's when the enemy plunges in, and I wanted to be here for you."

"Aw, Aunt Betty, that is so like you. I love you so much. To be honest, I'm glad you're here. I really do need your listening ear and wise words of encouragement right now. I'm supposed to have dinner at Matthew's tonight. Maybe you and I can have a heart-to-heart over those delicious blueberry muffins I've been smelling." Tracie was already heading toward the aroma of coffee and muffins.

Tracie poured a mug of coffee and sat at the table. She took a long drink and let the warm brew settle her before she began speaking. She took a muffin, still warm from the oven, broke it in half, slathered it with butter, and took a bite. Aunt Betty settled with her own coffee, added sugar and cream, and began stirring it as she looked up at Tracie.

"You said you believe the Lord has closed the door for you and Nicholas, is that right?" Aunt Betty asked.

"'Slammed the door' is more like it," Tracie said with a laugh.

"And do you feel like He has given you His blessing to proceed in your relationship with Matthew?" her aunt asked.

"I do, but …" She paused and took another bite of her muffin, not wanting it to get cold. "But I don't know if I'm ready. All this time has passed, and I had said over and over that if Nicholas ever left Jessica and wanted to come back, I'd let him, because I loved him that much. Even though he hurt me, there was a part of me that kept dreaming of how life used to be."

"Tracie, Nicholas is not that person anymore. He's changed. He doesn't even acknowledge God anymore. Is that the kind of man you want to spend the rest of your life with?" Aunt Betty asked.

Tracie shook her head and squeaked out a no.

Her aunt continued. "You can't begin the next chapter of your life if you keep rereading the last one. If you truly believe that God has put His blessing on your relationship with Matthew, let go of the past and start living again."

"I don't know if I can fully give my heart away right now," Tracie shared. "I'm so afraid of being hurt again." Tears began flowing down her cheeks.

Aunt Betty stood, walked over to Tracie, and put her arm around her. She said, "Come, Tracie, let's go to the sitting room." She kept her arm around Tracie as they walked and then sat with her on the love seat. Tracie laid her head on Aunt Betty's shoulder and sobbed.

Betty let her cry until she was done. Even then she didn't say a word for several moments. "Don't worry, Tracie. God is never blind to your tears. He's never deaf to your prayers or silent to your pain. He sees and he hears, and he will see you through this. You have to trust Him as you take the next step forward. If you're content with decorating, your family, and living life alone, be content in that. If you're not, you need to take a chance on love again, or your life will never change. Matthew loves you. I see it when he looks at you and smiles at you. His whole countenance changes when you walk into the room. There's a sparkle in his eyes. But this is a choice only you can make."

"Aunt Betty, I'm so glad you came home early. You've really helped me to open up and share my thoughts and feelings with you. You always seem to know what to say. You have so much wisdom."

"No, Tracie, this is God's doing. I asked Him to direct my words. He always hears and always answers when we call on him. Now, why don't you go up and get some rest before you get ready for your date with Matthew tonight?"

"It's not a date. It's just dinner," Tracie said.

"It's a date. Now, march," Aunt Betty said, pointing to the staircase.

Tracie kissed her aunt on the cheek, said "Yes, ma'am," and headed up to her room. She was quite exhausted. A nap would be a good thing. She would try to sleep for a couple of hours and would still have plenty of time to shower and get ready for her "date."

Chapter 21

*M*atthew was pulling into the parking area on his way back from the store when he spotted Tracie's car. His heart skipped a beat. He was looking forward to seeing her tonight. His dinner menu was planned, his house was spotless, and he had purchased some tiki lights for the deck along with a "deck-worthy" table and chairs for two. He had set up the table on the deck this morning before leaving to run errands. It was going to be a glorious spring evening. He wanted everything to be perfect, right down to presenting Tracie with the interlocking-gold-hearts necklace. He had rehearsed in his mind a thousand times what he wanted to say to her. Now the day had finally come.

His dinner menu consisted of a garden salad, grilled chicken, and a fresh blend of zucchini and squash, also grilled. There was mashed cauliflower with shredded cheddar and cream cheeses along with garlic toast. He had a light chardonnay to begin with, as well as iced tea or water. For dessert he had made a whipped strawberry mousse with a thin mint cookie crust.

Everything was done, and it was only noon. What was he going to do for the next five hours? Getting all the groceries in and preparing everything as much as he could had still left him with time on his hands. He turned on the radio and let it play softly while he sat in his favorite chair, opened his Bible, and began alternating between reading and praying.

Startled by a noise, Matthew sat up and tried to get his bearings. He had fallen asleep, he realized, and his Bible had slid off his lap and landed with a thud on the wood floor. After a few moments he realized what day it was, and he looked at the clock on the mantel. It was four thirty. He jumped up. Tracie would be there in less than an hour. He must have been more tired than he'd thought. He wasted no time in taking a shower, getting dressed, and firing up the grill.

Just as he was putting the basket of garlic bread on the table, he heard Tracie's footsteps on the stairs leading to the deck.

He walked over to greet her with a kiss on the cheek. "Hello!" he said. "You have perfect timing. I just put the bread on the table. Your dinner is served!" He bowed at the waist and stretched his arm out toward the table where a candle was encircled by fresh yellow and pink roses as well as baby's breath.

"You outdid yourself, kind sir," Tracie said with a smile. "Everything looks and smells wonderful."

He pulled out her chair and then took his seat across from her. He reached for her hand. "Shall we bless the food?" he asked.

"Absolutely," she replied.

Conversation over dinner was catch-up talk. Tracie shared about her new clients, the Malones, and Matthew told her he had been establishing a website to sell his driftwood tables. He had been searching other beaches down the coast to find more pieces and had gathered quite a collection, which was now stored in the area below his stilted house.

The late March evening had taken on a chill. They moved inside, cleaned up the dishes, and settled on the sofa in front of the fireplace, which was now blazing with the fire Matthew had started just before Tracie had arrived.

Matthew started the conversation. "So, Tracie, when we talked last night you said there was something you wanted to talk to me about."

"I did. I do," she replied. "After much prayer and fasting, I believe God has closed the door for me where Nicholas is concerned."

"Explanation, please. Did God tell you no, did you decide no, or did Nicholas change his mind?" Matthew's questions ran together.

"You are full of questions, Matthew Carrington," she said with a smile.

"It's only because I like you, Tracie," he replied.

"I like you too, Matthew," she said.

"Oh, that's not what I meant to say," he stammered.

"You *don't* like me then?" she asked.

"No. Yes. Tracie, I've been praying about the best way to tell you how I feel about you. I've rehearsed it in my mind a thousand times, and to tell you the truth, this isn't how it went in rehearsal."

Tracie just stared at him. He slid over closer to her on the sofa, took her hand, and began again. "Tracie, I know we've only known each other for a few months, but I feel like I've known you much longer. From the first time I saw you on the beach, I wanted to get to know you. In these past few months, I've become quite fond of you. I like you—a lot. I hope you feel the same way, because I've been praying that God would allow us to move forward in our relationship. Tracie, I have fallen in love with you. I want to date you, to court you properly."

"Matthew, I, um, I don't know what to say," Tracie responded, looking up at him.

"Please say yes," he said.

"I, um, yes. Yes, you may court me. I—I like you too, a lot. I—you—we can we take this slowly, Matthew, because I'm a little scared. Not scared of you. I—I'm pretty sure I'm falling in love with you, but I don't want to get hurt again." Tracie looked down at her lap.

Matthew took her face in his hands, looked her in the eye, and told her it was all going to be okay. "Slow is good. I want to give you all the time you need. I want to date you, court you, get to know you better. I love you, Tracie, and I believe the best is yet to come."

With her face still in his hands, he leaned forward and gently kissed her for the first time. Neither of them said a word. They sat back, and Tracie laid her head on his shoulder for a while. Finally she broke the silence. "Thank you, Matthew."

"For what?" he asked.

"For being so gentle and understanding with me," she said.

"I have something for you," he said as he reached into the carved wooden box on his coffee table and pulled out a velvet jewelry box. He opened the box to reveal the gold heart necklace. One heart was brushed gold, the other shiny. "Matthew, it's beautiful. But how did you know I would …" She left the sentence unfinished as she reached out and softly touched the gold hearts.

Matthew picked up where she left off. "I knew you would be willing to take our relationship to the next level, because I've been praying and fasting about it almost since the day I met you. As a matter of fact, I had this necklace and was going to tell you how I felt on Valentine's Day after we had dinner, but the timing just wasn't right."

"Oh, Matthew, I'm sorry," Tracie said. "You've been so patient and gentle with me."

"It was worth the wait," he said. "You said yes." He kissed her forehead.

Chapter 22

_Tracie had four days before her meeting with Sheri Malone to review and obtain approval for the rooms designs and decor for the three Malone children's rooms. She had gone over her notes for each room, and everything was entered into the design program on her computer.

Daniel's room was going to be a statement about Ohio State University, just as he wanted. Tracie had visited the website and fan club pages for Ohio State and had found a lot of inspiration and ideas. She had found a quilted spread, a replica of a football field. In the center was the Ohio State emblem and at the bottom was the team name: Buckeyes. She thought it would be clever to have a headboard handcrafted to look like goal posts on a football field. It all looked great on paper; she just hoped it wasn't too immature for Daniel's taste. It didn't look childish, but high school boys had their own opinions about things like that.

Mounted on the wall between the goals was an actual, official-size leather football. A two-tiered bedside table in the shape of the Ohio State Emblem was on one side of the extra-long twin bed. The only thing sitting on the glass top was Tony Dungy's book *A Quiet Strength*. It was an encouraging book for a young athlete. All the sports-themed rooms she'd decorated had included that book.

On the other side of the bed was a small dresser painted pewter gray with red knobs and a thin black line outlining the edges of the drawers. On top of the dresser sat a sleek black lamp with a soft-gray shade. The window coverings were wood blinds in the same soft gray. Tracie would make a wood cornice and cover it with the official Buckeye fabric.

Daniel's room was longer than it was wide, giving plenty of room at one end for a sitting area where he could have his friends over. Gracing that area were two slim black-leather chairs, one on either side of a small black-leather love seat. All of these she had found at a secondhand shop for a real bargain. The table in front of the sitting area was painted to match the pewter-gray dresser. There was a two-inch shelf inlaid into the table and covered by a glass top. Tracie had found Ohio State memorabilia to put under the glass. Her final touch would be a thirty-two-inch flat-screen television mounted on the wall.

Nikki's room was going to be fancy, with an antique cherry-wood four-poster bed, dresser, and grand mirror that had all belonged to her grandmother Rose. The details of the room were not all ironed out. Tracie planned to visit some of the antique shops downtown to decorate that space. The color scheme would be multiple shades of pink.

Tracie was working on the design for Josie's room when her phone rang, startling her. She looked at the phone before answering it and saw that it was Matthew's number. "Hey, you," she said as she swiped the phone to answer.

Matthew responded, "Hey yourself. What are you doing this beautiful Monday morning?"

"I'm in the middle of the design for little Josie Malone's room. This little girl knows what she wants. Now, if I can get it all on paper—or should I say, into my computer program—I'll be all set."

"Well, how about you take a break, pretty lady, and allow me to take you to an early lunch?" Matthew suggested.

"Matthew, it's already eleven o'clock. By the time you catch the noon ferry and drive up, I don't think it will be an early lunch," she said, laughing. "That would be a *late* lunch."

"It would have been a late lunch if I hadn't caught the ten o'clock ferry and wasn't sitting in your driveway right now," he said.

Tracie headed to the front room, looked out, and saw Matthew's truck. "What are you doing here?" she said as she headed out the front door.

"I told you, pretty lady. I want to take you to lunch."

"Aw, that is so sweet," she replied. "I didn't think I would see you again until Saturday."

"I wouldn't be doing a good job of courting you, now, would I, if I let a whole week go by without seeing you." Matthew winked at her.

"Come on in," she said. "I need to finish this one step on my design, turn off the computer, and get ready. She looked in the mirror she passed on the way back to the kitchen where she had been working. "Oh, my goodness, Matthew, I am a mess! I haven't even brushed my hair, put on makeup, or anything." Tracie frowned.

Matthew's only response was, "You look beautiful to me."

Chapter 23

*M*atthew took Tracie to the downtown Mattisson's City Grill where they enjoyed a nice summer salad. They were almost done with their lunch when Tracie raised her eyebrow, smiling as she looked across the table at Matthew. He said, "That look tells me your mind has been racing and an idea has just stopped your train of thought."

"You mean you've learned how my mind works already, Matthew?" she asked.

"Let's just say your facial expressions give you away sometimes," he said with a laugh.

"I was thinking, if you aren't too busy today, and since we're already downtown, would you mind taking me to some of the antique shops and secondhand stores to look for some things to go in Nikki Malone's room?" She looked up at him.

Matthew was smiling ear-to-ear.

"What?" Tracie said. "Why are you smiling like that, Matthew?"

"I enjoy being with you, Tracie," he said. "You make me happy, and I can't seem to stop smiling."

"Is that a yes then?" she asked.

"Of course! How could I deny you anything, Tracie? After all, I did come up to spend some time with you today."

"Thank you, Matthew," Tracie said. She excused herself and went to the ladies' room.

They decided to walk from Mattisson's on Main over to Second Street. As soon as they walked into one of the antique stores, Tracie spotted the wash basin and pitcher. It wasn't right in sight but was tucked into the far right corner of the small, crowded shop. She moved carefully through the aisles before stopping in front of it. Matthew was right behind her. She gently picked up the pitcher and said, "It's perfect."

"How do you do that?" Matthew questioned. "It's like you have a special radar sensor in that pretty little head of yours."

Tracie laughed. "I don't know. As soon as you opened the door for me, I spotted this out of the corner of my eye. Matthew, just look at it." The wash basin and pitcher were antique white with a scattered pattern of pink roses. The set was in really good condition, other than a chip or two, which were hardly noticeable.

She turned over the tag hanging from the pitcher's handle to see the price. "Whoa, $250," she said aloud. The tag did have an orange dot by the price. She looked around to see if there was a sign saying what the orange dot meant, but she didn't see any. She handed Matthew the pitcher and picked up the basin. "Let's go ask someone what the orange dot means. I hope it means it's a clearance item."

As Tracie approached a clerk, she saw that the woman's name tag said "Agnes." "Good afternoon, Agnes," Tracie said with a smile as if she was greeting a longtime friend.

Agnes looked up and replied, "Hello, sweetie. What can I help you with today?"

Tracie asked what the orange dot on the pitcher's price tag meant.

Agnes took the pitcher from Matthew and looked at the tag. "Let me see," she said, turning to her old-fashioned cash register where there was a small index card taped with colored dots and percentages written down. Agnes lifted the glasses that were hanging by a string around her neck and put them to her eyes. "Well, it looks like an orange dot means 40 percent off. Yes, that's it." She handed the pitcher back to Matthew. "Would you like me to wrap it up for you?" she asked as she turned to Tracie.

"Um, let me see," Tracie responded, calculating the discount in her head. "Yes, yes, I think I would like to take it."

Agnes took the basin from Tracie and turned back to Matthew for the pitcher. She took the price tag off and had started to ring up the order when Tracie heard her say, "Hmm."

"Is something wrong, Agnes?" Tracie asked.

"No, dear. I just turned the tag over and noticed yesterday's date on here. That's the date this item was supposed to be reduced to 60 percent off if it hadn't sold. That would make it a green-dot clearance," she said.

"Does that mean you'll mark it down another 20 percent for me today?" Tracie asked Agnes.

"Why, yes, sweetie," Agnes replied.

"Praise the Lord," Tracie said. "I just love it when God openly blesses me like this." She heard Matthew echo an *amen*.

It was nearly five o'clock when they returned to Tracie's house. She had accomplished a lot today. Not only had she found the pitcher and wash basin, but she'd also found a cherry-wood stand for it, along with a couple of antique pictures and lamps for Nikki's room.

Chapter 24

$\mathscr{S}$everal months had passed since Tracie had completed the Malone job. She had picked up small odd jobs since, nothing too time-consuming. Her focus had been on her novel and Matthew. Now she'd hit a major writer's block. Having a difficult time pulling her thoughts together to finish the novel, she decided to take a trip to Gatlinburg, Tennessee, the backdrop for her story. She hoped that being there would bring a breakthrough and that her thoughts would flow freely once again so she could finish the manuscript and send it to the publisher.

Her relationship with Matthew was serious. She knew it was just a matter of time before he proposed. She thought he was waiting for her book to go to press so they could begin their life together without any distractions.

Matthew encouraged her to go on her trip. He said he was going to miss her, but he wanted to see her fulfill her dream and become a published author. Her plan was to be away for three weeks. She had rented a small cabin in the mountains about twelve miles from Gatlinburg. She would stay there for ten days and then go to visit her dad before returning home. She talked to her dad every week by phone, but it had been two years since she'd seen him.

Tracie spent the first couple of days walking around, getting a feel for the town, the shops, and the eating establishments, taking notes and jotting down points of interest. She took the Gatlinburg

Sky Lift to view the quaint town. With ideas now running through her mind, she put pen to paper and was once again making progress on her novel.

The ringing of her phone broke her concentration. She usually turned the ringer off when she was writing for that very reason. She answered the call and found it to be a potential business deal. A few weeks back, she had met with a Mr. Delveccio. He had started a new business and wanted Tracie to partner in a joint venture with him and to use her skills to decorate his warehouse and office. The project had been put on the back burner while he worked out some of the financial issues. He wanted to make sure the business started with a solid foundation.

Matthew's plane landed. He had in hand the keys to the rental car and directions to the cabin Tracie was staying in. Thirty minutes later he was pulling into the driveway at the cabin. He knocked on the door and waited nervously. He had not told Tracie he was coming. He wanted to surprise her.

Tracie thought she heard a knock at the door. Thinking it odd, she rose from the chair and walked to the door. When she looked through the peephole, she saw Matthew standing there with a beautiful bouquet of flowers. She threw the door open, saying, "Matthew, what are you doing here?"

"Is that how you greet someone who has traveled miles through rough terrain, seeking high and low to find the love of his life?" he asked with a wink and a smile.

She broke into laughter. "Oh, my word, I'm just so surprised to see you standing here."

"I missed you so much, I decided to pay you a surprise visit," he said.

"You succeeded at that," she said. "I am surprised. Pleasantly surprised!"

After a couple of hours of conversation, they decided to go into Gatlinburg for dinner. Matthew said he would like to ride the sky lift before dinner, so that was their first stop.

Once they were high above the town, Matthew took her hand. Looking her in the eye, he said, "Tracie, it's no secret that I have fallen in love with you. You have brought new meaning to my life. You make my heart happy. I want to spend the rest of my days with you." Reaching into his pocket, he pulled out a small black-velvet box and flipped it open to reveal a beautiful white-gold solitaire engagement ring. "Tracie, I love you," he said. "Make me the happiest man on earth. Marry me."

Tracie looked at the ring and then at Matthew. Slowly she lifted her hand to his face and said softly, "I love you too. Yes. Yes, I will marry you."

They sealed their promise to marry with a kiss in the sky over Gatlinburg.

Later they had a nice dinner and then headed back to the cabin. Matthew told Tracie he had a room reserved in Pigeon Forge and would be back in the morning. As soon as Matthew left, Tracie picked up her phone and called Aunt Betty to share the news.

Tracie had just sent her manuscript off to the publisher via e-mail when Matthew arrived the next morning. She had stayed up half the night in order to complete it. Now she could move forward with wedding plans and a possible change in the direction of her business.

Chapter 25

$\mathcal{T}$racie spent her visit with her dad reminiscing. They went through boxes of old photographs and things that had been stored away in the attic since his move to Virginia. Tracie had thought her dad had given away all of her mother's belongings many years ago, so she was breathless when he pulled out a box, blew the dust off, and opened it to reveal hidden treasures. Her dad told her, "This box holds some of my most precious memories, Tracie. I want you to take it when you leave."

"Oh, Daddy," she said as she opened an oblong box holding a single string of pearls.

He proceeded to tell Tracie how he had worked extra hours leading up to his first Christmas with her mother so he could give her the pearl necklace. Tears flowed freely down his weathered cheeks.

There were other things in the box also: cards and love notes her parents had written each other. There was a small cloth doll that had Tracie's name stitched across the front of the homemade dress she wore. When Tracie lifted the doll out of the box, she remembered it. She looked over to where her dad had been sitting and discovered that he was no longer there.

Tracie left everything sitting where it was and went in search of her dad. He was not in the house, so she made her way to the barn. Walking through the open doors, she called out to him. "Daddy, are you okay?"

"I'm all right," he answered. "I was getting a little emotional up there, as I do every time I go up to the attic and take a trip down memory lane."

"I'm sorry it's still so painful for you, Daddy," she said as she walked over and gave him a hug. She sat on a stump across from him, and they talked for a while before heading back up to the house.

On the dinner menu were fried hamburger steaks, mashed potatoes, and fresh green beans from the garden. That had been one of Tracie's favorite meals as a child.

"You kept it," Tracie said as she sat at the round kitchen table watching her dad cook.

"Kept what?" he asked.

"The Tracie doll," she answered, looking down at her hands resting in her lap.

"I did. It was one of those things I just couldn't part with. When you decided you were too big for dolls and would not hear of just having it for a keepsake, I placed it in the box with all my special memorabilia. I can still see your momma sitting in her rocker by the fireplace, carefully sewing every stitch with love. She just knew she was having a girl, even though they didn't do ultrasounds back then to find out." He chuckled. "I would tease her and say, 'Mary, you may have to make a pair of trousers for that doll once the baby arrives.'" He looked at Tracie, who had tears running down her cheeks.

Walking over to her, he wiped the tears away with his thumbs. Tracie rose and wrapped her arms around him. She stayed like that until he said, "I think dinner is burning." They released their hug, and her dad turned back to the stove.

"Not too bad," he said, and they both laughed. "Now, tell me about the man who has won your heart."

"Oh, Daddy, he is so sweet and handsome. He loves the Lord, he loves the beach, and he likes working with wood. He has even helped me on some of my jobs with his carpentry skills."

"I would have liked to have met him before your wedding day," he said. "Your Aunt Betty has nothing but good to say about him, and she is a good judge of character. You deserve to be happy, Tracie, and by that peaceful smile you've been wearing, I believe you are. I love you, little girl." Then he turned and put their dinner on the table.

"I love you too, Daddy, and I'm so happy you'll be at the wedding."

The next morning, Tracie headed back home, cherishing the time she had shared with her dad. She felt that they had finally reconnected. Her dad had promised to see her at the wedding on November 26.

Chapter 26

It was the Saturday after Thanksgiving, and Tracie could not have asked for a more perfect wedding day. There was a gentle sea breeze without a cloud in the sky, and the temperature was in the low seventies. In the spot where Tracie usually laid her blanket on the beach, there stood a wrought-iron archway decorated in the colors of fall, including red chrysanthemums and sunflowers. A small crowd was gathering as family and a few friends waited for Tracie's arrival.

Matthew waited too, mingling with the guests.

Aunt Betty had done an amazing job preparing the beach house for guests. The fall decor made the place look like it had come right out of a magazine. Pumpkin spice candles were flickering in all the rooms, giving off the wonderful aroma of the season. Food—enough to feed an army—graced the tables and counters. The wedding cake was beautiful, with a deep-cream-colored frosting and fall flowers on the top and flowing down the side.

Tracie was admiring the decor when her aunt and her dad came into the sitting room. Tracie's dress was long, a cream-colored chiffon with long, sheer sleeves. She wore sandals in the same soft color. Her hair was pulled off to one side and was adorned with a red chrysanthemum.

Around her neck hung her mother's string of pearls. Her dad was beaming with pride and said, "Tracie, you look so much like your momma—breathtaking, beautiful."

"Daddy, that is so sweet of you to say," she responded.

"Well, it's true. Your momma would be so proud of the godly woman you have become. I know she is smiling down from heaven right now."

Aunt Betty stepped up to say, "We'd better be going. You don't want to be late for your own wedding, dear."

Tracie's aunt drove the golf cart to the path leading to the beach. She left Tracie and her dad there so she could walk down ahead and make sure everyone was in the right place. Then she started the CD player.

As the music began to fill the air, Tracie took her dad's arm. He asked, "Are you ready to do this, sweetheart?"

"I am, Daddy," she replied with a smile.

"Then let's not keep that young man waiting," he said as they began their walk down the path to the archway. Tracie had thought she would be extremely nervous, but she was filled with peace as they approached the area were the guests had gathered. Matthew looked so handsome in his brown suit. His cream-colored shirt was casually unbuttoned without the discomfort of a tie.

When Tracie and her dad stood in front of the pastor, the music stopped. The pastor greeted the guests and then turned to Tracie's dad and asked, "Who gives this woman to be married?"

Her dad responded, "Her daughter, her aunt, and I."

The pastor said a word of prayer and then asked that everyone be seated as the couple shared their vows.

"Matthew, will you please begin?" the pastor said.

"Yes," Matthew responded. "James 1:17 says that every good and perfect gift comes from above. Tracie, you are truly a gift from God. I promise to spend the rest of my life treating you as such. I promise to love you, encourage you, trust you, and be faithful to you. I will laugh with you in times of joy, and comfort you in times of sorrow. I will always cherish you and will never take you for granted. I will lead you and guide you as Christ leads me. We will build a life together far better than either of us could imagine alone." Placing the ring on her finger, he continued. "Please accept this ring as a symbol of our covenant and my love for you until God calls us home."

The pastor then looked at Tracie. "Tracie, will you continue by stating your vow to Matthew?"

"Yes," she said. "Matthew, you are the answer to my prayers, my gift from God. I will spend the rest of my life thanking God for loving me enough to send me his best. I promise to love you, encourage you, trust you, and be faithful to you. I will laugh with you in times of joy, and comfort you in times of sorrow. I will cover you in prayer. I will care for you and never take you for granted." Placing the ring on his finger, she continued. "Please accept this ring as a symbol of our covenant and my love for you until God calls us home."

The pastor asked, "Matthew, do you take Tracie to be your wife, to love her, to honor her, and to keep her as long as you both shall live?"

"I do," he responded.

"Tracie," said the pastor, "do you take Matthew to be your husband, to love him, to honor him, and to keep him as long as you both shall live?"

"I do," Tracie said.

The pastor looked up and said, "God has joined these two together. Let no one ever come between them. I now pronounce you husband and wife. Matthew, you may kiss your bride."

Tracie's dad was the first to congratulate the newlyweds, followed by Ella, Jason, and Bailey. Aunt Betty gave them a quick hug and hurried off to be ahead of the guests arriving at the beach house.

Alice was next in line. "You are absolutely glowing, girlfriend," she said. "I'm so happy for you. You too, Matthew. You'd better take good care of her, or you will have my wrath upon you!" She winked and kissed each of them on the cheek.

When everyone had arrived at the beach house for the reception, the celebration began. Toasts were made, the cake was cut, and everyone was engaged in conversation. Suddenly Tracie realized that she hadn't seen Matthew for a while. About that time, Aunt Betty called for Tracie. "Tracie, dear, there is someone out front asking for you."

"Who is it?" she asked.

"I think you need to come and see for yourself," her aunt responded.

Tracie got to the front door and stopped in her tracks. She couldn't believe what see was seeing.

There was the most gorgeous white horse she had ever seen. Sitting atop the horse was a knight in shining armor. He dismounted, walked up to Tracie, swept her off her feet, and remounted with her.

Tracie began to call out for Matthew, but at that point the knight raised his face shield—and she saw Matthew's smiling face.

Relieved, she leaned back against him. He turned the horse toward the beach, and the newlyweds rode off into the sunset.

Printed in the United States
By Bookmasters